"Don't fight it, Alex," Jake said softly

With that his lips possessed hers firmly, and his arms tightened their hold. *I can't let him keep doing this to me,* Alex thought, trying to ignore her pounding heart. Taste him, hold him, her heart seemed to say seductively. Put your arms around him.

As if in a dream, Alex obeyed, all of her senses responding so acutely they seemed magnified. There was the firm pressure of his body against her. *He wants me,* she thought dizzily. When his hand slid inside her blouse, she drew in her breath sharply.

Oh, Lord, what am I thinking of? she wondered as Jake pulled his head back and smiled drowsily at her.

Katherine Arthur is full of life. She describes herself as a writer, research associate (she works with her husband, a research professor in experimental psychology), farmer, housewife, proud mother of five and a grandmother to boot. The family is definitely full of overachievers. But what she finds most interesting is the diversity of occupations the children have chosen—sports medicine, computers, finance and neuroscience (pioneering brain tissue transplants), to name a few. Why, the possibilities for story ideas are practically limitless.

Books by Katherine Arthur

HARLEQUIN ROMANCE
2755—CINDERELLA WIFE
2821—ROAD TO LOVE

Forecast of Love
Katherine Arthur

Harlequin Books

TORONTO • NEW YORK • LONDON
AMSTERDAM • PARIS • SYDNEY • HAMBURG
STOCKHOLM • ATHENS • TOKYO • MILAN

Original hardcover edition published in 1987
by Mills & Boon Limited

ISBN 0-373-02905-5

Harlequin Romance first edition May 1988

CHAPTER ONE

'ALEX, you didn't! You bit the world's most eligible bachelor on the leg?'

'That's right.' Alexis Faraday fought to keep a straight face as she asked, 'Isn't anyone going to say something about my taste in men?'

The two friends with whom Alexis was having lunch in the employees' cafeteria of the Northern Grain Consortium, groaned 'Oh, Alex!' in unison, their faces contorted with comic torture at her pun. Alex burst out laughing, glad for momentary relief of the tension that had begun to mount in anticipation of her one o'clock meeting with the President of the company.

'Judging from this article, he had it coming,' said Madge Jones, a staunch advocate of women's rights. She gestured toward the magazine which lay on the table between them.

Sarah Loftus gave Madge a sceptical look. 'I'll bet if you could get your hands on that handsome hunk you wouldn't bite him. I know I wouldn't.' She leaned forward and smiled encouragingly at Alex. 'I didn't know you knew Jake Jensen. When did it happen?'

'A long time ago,' Alex replied. 'At the time I thought he had it coming, too.'

The two women stared at her, their eating suspended.

'All right,' Alex said with a sigh, 'I guess I'll have to explain my lurid past. You see, the Jensens had a huge cottage at Tamarack Lake, where my grandparents, cottage was...is. Both of my grandparents are dead now, so I haven't been there in years. Jake Jensen was on his summer break from college, doing the big football hero routine with all of the local girls. Even then he obviously thought he was the world's best catch. I was only fourteen, still just a stick, with no figure and braces on my teeth...no one Jake would notice.' She paused and pointed to the picture in the magazine. 'He always went for bosomy females like the one in the picture with him. He liked to wrestle around with them on the diving raft in the lake, and they just loved it when he'd pick them up and throw them in. I had a terrific crush on him, and I was terribly envious of those girls with their cute, sexy figures. One day I was hanging around the raft, taunting him to get his attention. I started to climb up the ladder, and he said something like "Get lost, pest," and then took one big foot and knocked me back into the lake.'

'What did you say?' Sarah asked, as Alex paused to take a bite of her sandwich.

'I don't recall. You know the kind of sparkling repartee a fourteen-year-old is capable of. Anyway, my adolescent ego was badly bruised, and when I came to the surface again, I was boiling mad. I sneaked on to the raft, crawled up behind Jake, and chomped down on the calf of his leg. That really got his attention!' Alex smiled wryly, remembering the fury in Jake Jensen's deep blue eyes as he had whirled around.

'What did he do?' came the prompt from Madge.

'He picked me up like a sack of flour, swatted my bottom a couple of times, and threw me about twenty feet out into the lake. That part was fun, but I was afraid to try to get him to do it again. He said if I didn't stay off the raft for the rest of the afternoon he'd drown me. And that, alas, is the end of my story. Before the end of that summer his mother died, his father went into a depression, and Jake went off to become Mr Jenstar. I haven't seen him since.'

'How sad,' Sarah said with a sigh. 'If he'd been around when you grew up to be as pretty as you are now, something romantic might have happened between you.'

'I doubt it,' Alex said, nodding toward the magazine. 'I can't imagine getting involved with someone who'd say something like that.'

Alex was referring to the article below the picture of Jake Jensen, over which Madge had earlier been clucking in righteous disapproval. The article reported tersely, 'Jake Jensen, head of the giant multi-national corporation known as Jenstar, was taken to task last week by the National Women's Caucus for his statement, "There is only one position suitable for a woman," overheard at a reception for trade representatives from the European Bloc. He denied that it had any relevance to policy at Jenstar, but NWC is not convinced, pointing to the glaring lack of women in executive positions at the firm.'

'I wouldn't mind working for him in almost any position,' Sarah said dreamily.

'Sarah! Shame on you,' Madge exclaimed, shocked.

'Well, I wouldn't,' Sarah retorted, ignoring Madge's liberated glare. 'He's gorgeous.'

'And that's why he can get away with what he does,' Madge said coldly.

Sarah shrugged. 'I doubt if he can singlehandedly undermine the cause of women's lib.' She turned her attention back to Alex. 'Did he look that good when you knew him?'

'Not quite,' Alex replied, studying the picture more closely. 'He carried more weight when he played football. Who's the bosomy redhead with him?' Her question referred to the scantily clad woman staring soulfully at

Jake Jensen, her tiny hands clutching his impressive biceps.

'That's Lorna Beauregard, the country singer,' Sarah replied quickly. 'Don't you recognise her? They're supposed to be a hot item right now. Practically engaged.'

'I'm not much of a country fan,' Alex said, dabbing her mouth with her napkin and then taking a deep breath. 'I guess I'd better get going. I don't want to be late for my meeting with our exalted President.' She felt a tightness in her stomach at the thought, but smiled at her friends brightly. 'Wish me luck.'

'You don't need luck. You're sure to get the promotion,' Sarah said with an encouraging smile. 'I just hope you'll still have lunch with us now and then when you're the Vice President for Economic Forecasting.'

'Don't worry, I won't let it go to my head.' Alex made a wry face. 'However, in case you hadn't noticed, there aren't any women execs here, either.'

'You'll be the first,' Madge said loyally, although the lack of conviction in her voice did not escape Alex's notice.

'Sure you will...but what will you do if they give it to Noel Smith instead?' Sarah asked, artlessly injecting the name of the one person who might stand between Alex and the vice presidency.

Alex sighed. 'At first I tried not to think about that, then I decided I'd better. I've got my résumé all ready to send out and my resignation ready to hand in. If I don't get the promotion...I'll quit.'

'Alex!' Madge exclaimed, frowning. 'You mustn't. You should stay and fight it out. You're the best qualified, and you know it.'

'I know I am, but I've been fighting the problem here for three years now and I'm tired of it. There are plenty of opportunities for someone with my qualifications in places that treat women more fairly. Besides, now that Mother and Greg are gone there's nothing to keep me in Minneapolis-St Paul.' She pushed her chair back and stood up. 'Well, here I go.'

She repeated that phrase to herself a scant two hours later when, dressed in jogging clothes, she burst through the screen door of her apartment into the hot July afternoon, determined to run until she was sure she would neither start screaming like a maniac nor crying like a baby. They had given the promotion to Noel Smith, that miserable little incompetent, who came to her at least ten times a day with problems he couldn't solve!

Upon hearing the news, Alex had handed in her resignation with as much dignity as she could muster, managing to state her objections quite calmly in spite of an almost overwhelming urge to stuff her resignation down the President's throat.

Think about what you're going to do next, instead of going over that scene, Alex told herself as she pounded along the pavement in a long-legged stride, her blonde hair flying behind her. But her mind seethed with bitter, angry resentment. Her achievements spoke for themselves. There was only one possible reason Noel had been chosen over her. He was a male, with a wife and family to support! Apparently, even in this day and age, there were still people—notably the board of directors of the Northern Grain Consortium—who thought that made all the difference!

Men! Alex scowled and mopped her perspiring face with the handkerchief she carried. All they ever did was let her down. Her father had deserted them some ten years ago; her college heart-throb had wandered away when Alex had refused to give up the idea of a career in favour of marriage; her brother, Greg, had headed for California to join their mother and try to break into the movies as soon as he'd finished college. Not that she resented his leaving, but it was lonely without him. There weren't any men in her life now. Hadn't been for years. She had worked so hard, taking extra courses, trying to get ready for the promotion she was sure would come. She thought of her lunch-time revelations and grimaced. Now she'd probably be remembered at Northern Grain for ever, not as the bright young economist, but as the woman who once bit Jake Jensen! And even Jake Jensen had thrown her back like an undersized fish!

Alex completed her circuit down Como Avenue to the park and back, dripping and panting from the heat. Two bounds took her on to the porch of the big old house where she and Greg had shared a downstairs apartment until he'd left. She could hear her phone ringing, and quickly ran through to her kitchen, leaping over Murphy, her cat, who let out a yowl of protest at being so nearly squashed by his mistress's flying feet.

'Hello?' she gasped, grabbing the receiver from its wall cradle. 'Oh, Mother! Hi! No, I'm all right. I've been out jogging... But if you didn't think I'd be home this early, why did you call?' Sometimes her mother's logic escaped her completely! 'Oh, you've met a fascinating man. That's nice.'

Alex held the receiver on her shoulder, reaching to find some ice-cubes in the refrigerator and then fix a glass of iced water. If Darlene Faraday was having another affair, this could take a while. Ever since Alex's father had left, her mother had been looking for a replacement. Her meanderings reminded Alex of nothing so much as a confused honey bee, bumbling from one plastic flower to another in search of nectar that wasn't there. When would she ever learn?

'What was that, Mother? I was running some water in a glass, I didn't catch it...the Faraday cottage? Yes, I remember it's supposed to be auctioned this summer. Something about Grandma's will, wasn't it? You have to go there to get the family keepsakes and see if it needs cleaning? Oh! You want me to go there? Sure. I'd love to!' What a wonderful respite that would be right now! 'I can go right away. Tomorrow...No, I'm not on vacation, I'm unemployed...That's right. I quit Northern. It's a long story.'

Alex rolled her eyes upward as her mother exclaimed her distress, then quieted her and told her the facts. 'No, I don't mind going at all,' she reassured her again when she had finished. 'I'm going to send out my résumés tonight, but I'll have a few days before I need to worry about anyone pounding on my door, begging me to come and work for them... No, probably New York. That's where all the big financial houses are.'

'Phew,' Alex said, letting her breath out in a rush after her mother had finally hung up. At least Darlene sounded happy this time. So often, it was the story of another sad affair's end. A fascinating man, she had said, but she hadn't mentioned his name. Oh, well, she'd find out soon enough.

'Murphy,' Alex said, as the big, spotted cat came and curled around her legs, meowing piteously for his dinner, 'you are going to have to wait until I have a shower. But I've got good news for you. Tomorrow, we're going to Tamarack Lake, and there are fish there. Lots of fish. And I'll catch some just for you. Think you'll like that?'

'Yow,' replied Murphy, licking his chops thoughtfully.

In the morning Murphy rode curled up atop a pile of bedding in the back seat of Alex's car as she drove north toward the lovely lake, nestled in the pine forests of northern Minnesota. It was hazy and hot and the air conditioning in her car was not very effective, but the relief she felt at getting away from the frustration and disappointment of yesterday made her whistle softly to herself, the discomfort only minor. The soft scent of pine brought back memories of carefree childhood summers. There hadn't been many times like those in recent years. Her single-minded dedication to her work had prevented her from taking a real vacation. This time it was going to be different. She was going to do nothing but swim and fish and do whatever cleaning was necessary.

'We're almost there,' she told Murphy, when he became restive near midday. 'I can see the Tamarack Lake water tower.'

They drove through the little resort town on the east side of the seven-mile-long lake, then north past the Lakeside Inn, its long stretch of beach the site of Jake Jensen's former exploits with the young ladies of the area. They passed the grassy expanse of land where the Jensens' huge 'cottage' had stood before the spectacular fire which had burned it to the ground, then turned on to the gravel road which led along the north end of the lake. Finally, they took an almost concealed lane through a stand of pines, stopping by a silvery cedar cottage with green shutters and a big screened porch overlooking its own little beach.

'And here we are.' Alex opened the door, Murphy bounded out, and she got out slowly and stretched. It felt like a vacation already. If only Grandma Faraday were still here to fuss over her and bake one of her marvellous apple pies, it would be perfect.

Alex sighed and chased away the twinge of sadness that thoughts of her grandmother brought by swinging into action, opening the cottage, hurrying around to fling up the windows and let the breeze in to sweep away the mustiness, then beginning to carry in her supplies. The bedding she carried upstairs, to the little room under the eaves she had always occupied, its dormer windows offering a wide view of the lake and the tiny, uninhabited island which lay about half a mile south. There was always good fishing near the island, Alex recalled, leaning on the windowsill, drinking in the lake-fresh breeze and the beautiful sight of sunlight reflecting like diamonds from the waves. Tomorrow morning she would row over there and try it. If, that was, there was still a boat on the place that didn't leak like a sieve! She had better check that out right away.

A few minutes later, Alex had discovered a small aluminium boat and oars in the shed behind the cottage. She dragged it around to the front, floated it briefly to check for leaks, then beached it again.

'There,' she said in satisfaction, wiping her grimy hands on her jeans. 'Watch out, fish. I'll be coming after you in the morning.'

She spent the rest of the afternoon industriously scrubbing, with occasional pauses to dispose of the dead fish that Murphy scavenged on the shore and brought to the doorstep for her approval. During the evening she went through several boxes of dusty old books that she had found in a cupboard. One, its pages brittle with age, was a combination ledger and diary. She started to read it, increasingly absorbed by the insights the entries gave into the early days at Tamarack Lake. One item was particularly interesting. It said, 'Loaned a hundred dollars to Carl Jensen. He plans to start a general store in Tamarack. Sure could use one.' How fascinating! The official beginning of one of the world's biggest corporations! And a Faraday had got them started.

'I wonder if Carl paid the loan back,' Alex mused aloud to Murphy. She did some quick calculations. At five per cent interest, the debt would be over ten thousand dollars by now. 'What do you suppose Jake Jensen would do if I sent him a photocopy of this item and a bill?' she asked the cat.

Murphy raised his head and yawned tremendously.

'I think you're right,' Alex said with a chuckle, rubbing him behind his ears. 'Let's go to bed. I'm going to get up early and go fishing.'

The clock radio which Alex had brought awakened her before dawn to a combination of rock and roll and the crackling of static. She rubbed her eyes sleepily. Static. That meant storms in the area. Should make for good fishing. She pulled on a pair of cut-off jeans and a T-shirt, then added an old khaki long-sleeved shirt as protection against the early morning chill. She wound her hair into a knot on top of her head and plopped a battered straw hat from her grandfather's wardrobe on top for luck.

'Fishing-pole, tackle box, cushion, net . . . I guess I've got everything,' she enumerated before going out the door. 'No, Murphy, you stay in and catch some mice. I heard some scurrying around last night. I'll be back soon.'

In minutes Alex had her gear in the boat and was pushing off from shore in the misty greyness of first light that her grandfather had loved so well. 'That's when the big ones hit,' he had always said. And, she thought as she pulled on the oars, he had always said the best bass pool was on this side of the island. She'd try her luck there first.

The lake was glassy and calm, the air still. Only the sound of her oars slicing the water and the creak of the oar locks disturbed the quiet as Alex rowed swiftly toward the island, her heart beating a little faster with the pleasant anticipation of casting her lure and feeling the tug of a strike. Near the island she slowed her pace and drifted along the rocky north side, remembering the fanciful names that she and Greg had bestowed on different places when they played their pirate games there. Pirate's Plank was a flat rock at the top of a little cliff, protruding over the water by a few feet. Shipwreck Cove was a little indentation where the bottom was strewn with sharp rocks. Just beyond was the Devil's Drowning Pool, which was also, if one were fishing, the bass pool.

Here, beneath the surface of the water, a rocky ledge dropped off to a depth of ten feet or so and a gnarled old oak tree leaned precariously toward the water's edge from above. Quietly Alex dropped her anchor and prepared her fishing-line. Carefully she took aim and cast, then reeled the frog-like lure back in so that it jerked along in realistic fashion. Over and over she repeated her motions.

'Got one!' she breathed at last, as the lure disappeared from sight and the end of her pole bent beneath the strain. It was a big one, too, but she had been well trained and in minutes had it alongside the boat and scooped it up in her net. 'Nice work,' she told herself approvingly, holding the large bass up to admire it before putting it on the stringer attached to her boat frame. She went back to fishing, soon catching another good-sized fish.

With the first rays of the sun, a breeze sprang up. Alex cast again and again with no luck. Just one more try, she told herself, and then I'll quit. Maybe if I lay it right by the shore...

'Oh, damn!' she said aloud. Whether it was the breeze or her eye was off she wasn't sure, but the lure had caught in the branches of the old oak tree. She gave it a jerk, but nothing happened. She would have to pull up anchor and get in closer. As she did so she noticed a speedboat coming around the east end of the island. Wonderful! she thought drily. That would set her boat to rocking with its wake. She hated speedboats, the bane of the real fisherman's existence. Giving a pull on the oars, she drifted in toward the shore, turning her attention to the trapped lure. If she stood up and gave a pull toward the right...

'What the hell do you think you're doing?' a deep voice, gravelly with displeasure, shouted above the hollow sounds of a big inboard engine idling behind her.

'Fishing for tree bass, what's it look like?' she snapped without looking back, trying to keep her balance in the rocking boat. She gave another tug on her line, still with no results.

'Here. Let me do it.'

'No! I don't need...' Alex turned her head at the sound of a splash and then someone sloshing through the water toward her. She froze, and her heart seemed to do a strange set of gymnastics in her chest as she recognised him. It was Jake Jensen, all six foot plus of him, looking about as friendly as he had the day she'd sunk her teeth into his leg!

CHAPTER TWO

ALEX could not seem to move. She suddenly felt small, shapeless, skinny, and completely overwhelmed by the sight of the towering, broad-shouldered man with the fierce scowl on his face, pushing his way determinedly toward her through the water in now very wet blue jeans and a striped cotton shirt.

'My God, a female,' Jake Jensen growled, as he reached the bass pool and subjected Alex to a brief, scathing look. He stuck out a long arm out toward her. 'Just hand me your rod, young lady, and...'

'Watch out! You're going to fall off...'

But before Alex could finish her warning, Jake Jensen had stepped off the underwater ledge. Feeling himself sinking he grabbed reflexively for Alex's arm, pulling her into the hole with him and sending her boat flying forward on to the rocky shore with a crash as her feet slipped out from under her.

The plunge into the icy water completely eliminated Alex's previous stupefaction. 'You idiot!' she spluttered as she surfaced to see Jake Jensen's head a few feet away, a surprised look on his face. 'You haven't improved one darn bit, have you?' She paddled swiftly to the shore, retrieving her hat and fishing-pole as she went, and then waded out to stand dripping and glaring at the man who had followed her.

'What's that supposed to mean?' Jake glared back in what Alex decided was a manner designed to intimidate her.

She jerked her chin up at him defiantly. 'It means that my most vivid memory of you in years past involved your kicking me off the diving raft at Lakeside. Now you've not only dunked me, but you've managed to make a hole in my boat and get my tackle all wet. I hope you're satisfied!' She scowled at him and then turned to investigate the damage to her boat and lift her dripping tackle box from its water-logged interior.

'Who the devil are you, and what are you doing here?' Jake demanded, his eyes raking Alex up and down as if she were a criminal in a line-up, while she opened her tackle box and assessed the damage to its contents. She was trying to decide whether to answer him or invent some fictitious identity when suddenly his frown faded and his mouth quirked up in a one-sided smile. 'Wait a minute, I remember you. You're Alexis Faraday, the skinny little blonde who bites.' His eyes did another circuit, more slowly this time, from her wide-set blue eyes, down the warm curves revealed by her drenched clothes, and then back to her face. 'You seem to have improved quite a bit, except for your wardrobe,' he said, looking amused at Alex's flush of discomfort as he asked, 'Do you still bite?'

'I was dressed for fishing, not swimming,' she retorted, surprised that Jake Jensen would remember that incident, considering the legions of women who must have scratched and clawed at him in the intervening years. 'And I only bite when I'm extremely aggravated.' Which I am fast becoming, she added to herself, as Jake subjected her to an even more detailed appraisal, with eyes which now had some interesting lines around them, as if he did that sort of smiley I-can-imagine-you-without-your-clothes-on thing very often.

'Well, I think we can eliminate one source of aggravation for you pretty fast,' Jake said, glancing up at the lure in the tree. 'But tell me, Alex, if you wanted to see me again, why didn't you just come to my door and knock instead of pretending to fish and then throwing a lure into a tree to set off my alarm?'

Come to his door? Alarm? That made no sense at all. 'What door?' Alex demanded. 'And what alarm?'

'Oh, come on, Alex,' Jake said with a knowing smile. 'I bought the island and built my earth cottage here two years ago. I find I need an alarm system to keep trespassers away. If you don't know about it, you're the only Tamarack resident who doesn't.'

Alex cocked her head and stared at Jake Jensen with incredulity. The man's ego was fantastic, and his comment about her fishing revealed a positively stone-age mentality! 'I haven't been here since my grandfather died and my grandmother went into a rest home five years ago,' she said coldly. 'Sorry to disappoint you, but I didn't know. I was fishing to catch fish!' She marched over to her now submerged boat and untied the stringer, lifting the two big bass into view. 'What do you call these?'

Jake's black eyebrows rose in two arches. 'Nice bass,' he said. 'Now that you know I'm here, you can bring them with you when you come calling. They were on my property, you know.'

'Your property?' Did he think he owned half the lake? 'I didn't know you could claim territorial waters along with your island. If it comes to that, then I claim prior possession. I used to be queen of the Tamarack Lake pirates, and this island was my domain, bass pool and all.' Oh, lord, why did I say that? Alex wondered, as

Jake roared with laughter. He made her feel like a stupid fourteen-year-old again.

'All right, Queen Alexis,' Jake said, grinning at her and making her feel more uncomfortable by the minute, 'I'll let it go this time, if you'll agree to share them with me for dinner tonight. That's a better invitation than most of my would-be callers get.'

Alex glared, restraining an impulse to swing the heavy fish and whop Jake Jensen on the side of his handsome face with them. 'I don't want any invitation,' she said frostily. 'I am planning on sharing the fish with my cat. Now if you will just hold this...' she set the fish down and thrust her fishing-rod out toward Jake '... I think I can climb up there and loosen that lure.'

'Let me get it,' he said dismissively, making a move toward the shelf upon which the tree grew.

'Good grief, Jake, you'd break that rotten old tree right off,' Alex said with a shake of her head, intercepting him. 'Just hold this up and tighten the line slowly so the lure doesn't come flying down and get stuck in something else.'

Jake frowned and muttered something about stubborn women, but this time he reluctantly took the rod and Alex cast off her heavy, drenched khaki shirt and bounded up the ledge, grasped a small branch and swung herself upward, flinging one leg over the first large limb and levering herself up on to it. Then she reached for a higher branch, stood up and worked her way carefully outward until she could reach the tangled lure.

'Here it comes,' she said, loosening it from the tree.

'Got it.' Jake reeled it in and then leaned the rod against the bank. 'Now get down from there before you fall and break something.'

'I am not about to fall,' Alex snapped disgustedly. She started to work her way back down the branch, glancing down at Jake, who was standing with arms folded across his broad chest, his legs, encased in clinging wet jeans, planted apart. He looked like some medieval war lord about to give his serfs and vassals marching orders, Alex thought as she bent to grasp the branch. Suddenly there was a cracking sound, and simultaneously a cry from Jake.

'Look out!'

It was only a short fall as the branch gave way, but Jake's cry had startled her and Alex landed awkwardly, taking a few stumbling steps before catching her foot and twisting to land with a bone-racking jolt on the rocky shore.

'Are you all right?' Jake cried, hurrying over and bending to peer down at her anxiously.

Alex pushed herself gingerly to a sitting position, ignoring the hand that Jake held out toward her, and felt herself where her bottom had landed on a sharp rock. 'I don't think I'll want to sit down for a while,' she said, wincing.

'Let me help you,' Jake said impatiently. He reached down and lifted her with one hand beneath each armpit.

'Wait a minute. My foot's caught,' Alex said, trying to push Jake away and instead lurching forward against his chest, a sharp knife of pain surging up her leg as she tried to pull it free. She looked up at Jake, whose arms had tightened around her and who was now staring at her with a bemused little smile. 'I am not making a pass at you,' she snapped, pushing at his chest again. 'My foot is stuck between some rocks.'

Jake's smile widened. 'I was just thinking that this is a perfect opportunity to give you that kiss you wanted so badly the day you bit me.'

'Oh, no, it isn't,' Alex said, trying to wriggle free of Jake's grasp. Did this egomaniac think she'd been waiting all these years for his attentions? 'You're about thirteen years too late. Not only that, but my ankle hurts and I am becoming extremely aggravated!'

'Uh-oh, I'd better be careful,' Jake said, doing his one-sided smile again. He released Alex and crouched before her, pushing and prodding at the rocks until at last her foot was free. 'There,' he said, standing again just as a spate of huge raindrops came pelting down around them.

'Now what?' Alex demanded, glancing up at the skies and trying to ignore the fact that she was getting another going-over from those ridiculously long-lashed, deep blue eyes. She shivered a little. The wind was coming up, too. 'Are you just going to stand there?' she snapped, as he continued to stare at her.

'I am until you tell me, Alexis Faraday,' Jake replied, unfolding his arms and planting his hands on his hips, 'just how you plan on getting back to your cottage to share those fish with your cat unless I take you there? Your boat obviously has a large hole in it. And, since I refuse to take you unless you'll agree to come for dinner...' he glanced over his shoulder at the sound of heavy, rolling thunder '...you and your fish may have to sit here and endure quite a storm.'

'Oh, all right,' Alex said, with an impatient sigh. Good heavens, but the man was persistent!

'Come on, then,' he said, looking upward as the rain began to pelt down in earnest. 'We'd better get a move on.'

Alex took a step, then stumbled forward, catching herself with her hands. 'Darn! I must have twisted my ankle,' she cried in frustration. 'And with all the work I have to do!'

'Hold these,' Jake said, rounding up Alex's tackle box, rod and fish, and then scooping her up into his arms. Thunder crashed nearby, leaving a trail of deep, echoing vibrations. 'We're going to have to high-tail it for my place,' he said, as the increasing wind whipped his black hair across his forehead. 'This storm is coming in fast.'

'Oh, no!' Alex wailed, thinking of Murphy's terror of storms and the windows she had left open. But a glance at the sky told her that Jake was right. A rolling band of white clouds that seemed so close she could touch it was proceeding swiftly along ahead of a purplish sky. Those were the wind clouds that sometimes preceded a violent thunderstorm. At any moment, gale-force winds would strike the lake, whipping its placid surface into frothing waves.

Jake started back toward his boat, picking his way with some difficulty across the boulder-strewn bottom. He looked down at Alex, who was watching their progress anxiously, hoping that Jake wouldn't trip and dunk her again. 'What are you so worried about?' he asked, cocking a disdainful black eyebrow at her. 'Afraid I'm going to drop you?'

'Yes,' she answered, grinning as he became tight-lipped in displeasure at her reply. Just then he staggered forward, but caught the side of the big boat in time to avoid falling. 'Nice work. Graceful,' she said, and he gave her a smile that was more like a grimace as he lifted her upwards.

Alex dropped her gear into the boat and then pulled herself over the side and into the wide, cushioned back seat. Jake climbed in, settled himself behind the steering wheel, and started the engine, backing up for a short distance before turning and gunning the motor for all it was worth. If we had tyres, they'd be screeching, Alex thought wryly, remembering that a younger Jake Jensen had frequently 'burned rubber' when starting up from a corner in his flashy Porsche, in order to impress the local maidens fair.

She hung on tightly as Jake skirted the island in a wide arc, the speeding boat leaving a huge rooster tail behind it. In minutes, they were coming up slowly beside an elegant little dock.

'Just sit there for a minute,' Jake said, after he had helped Alex out of the boat and on to the dock. 'I've got to tie this down tight.' In the silence that followed the killing of the boat's engine she could hear the ominous roll of continuous thunder to the west. There was an icy edge to the gusts of wind that came with increasing frequency.

Jake moved swiftly, attaching ropes to both the front and rear of the boat. 'There,' he said, as he finished. 'Let's go. Come on, Bozo,' he called to a large German shepherd dog, who had come loping down to the dock to greet them. He picked Alex up again, and as if someone had suddenly cried out 'Now!' a blast of wind hit with a force that made him stagger.

Alex curled against him, trying to make herself small and offer the least wind resistance possible. Jake struggled the short distance up a flagstone path to a wall of glass, which Alex had little time to admire as the front of his cottage, embedded in the hillside. He tugged open a sliding door, squeezed inside, and then closed it rapidly. 'Whew! This is going to be some storm.' He looked down at Alex, who was still curled against his chest, wondering bemusedly to herself if this was how a cave woman had felt when a cave man rescued her from charging lions. But this was some fancy cave!

'Still not sure you want to pay me a visit?' he asked, shifting Alex in his arms so that he could give her the full benefit of his smile, the deep smile lines and thick black lashes managing to make them appear very warm in spite of their cool, dark blueness.

Oh, so now that he thinks he's got me trapped here he's going to really turn on the charm, Alex thought, a little shiver of nervousness accompanying her assessment of the new gleam in those midnight-blue eyes.

'No, I'm not,' she replied, pushing herself away from Jake's chest. 'Especially now, since my cat's home alone and he'll be terrified, and I left some of the windows open. I didn't need any more of a mess to clean up.' She frowned at Jake. 'You can put me down now. I think I can hop along on a smooth floor.'

'Mmph,' Jake replied, which Alex assumed meant 'no', for he carried her toward a round oak dining-table and deposited her carefully on a chair. 'Let's have a look at your ankle,' he said, glancing up in concern as Alex let out a yelp of pain. 'What's hurting you now?'

'I sat down on a sharp rock out there,' she replied coldly. 'Remember?'

'Mmm, yes. Nasty fall. You should have let me get the lure.' He slid a meaningful glance in Alex's direction.

'Oh, sure,' Alex said with a derisive snort. 'You'd be lying out there now with the whole tree on top of you.'

Jake shrugged, sat down in another chair and picked up Alex's foot. He removed her shoe, which deposited a puddle of water on to the gleaming tiled floor. 'Can you move the ankle at all?' he asked, holding Alex's chilly foot in one large hand and carefully feeling the bones with the tips of his fingers.

'Yes, but it hurts to do it,' Alex replied, flexing her ankle a little and grimacing. She leaned forward and studied her ankle. 'I think it's just an old-fashioned sprain. I'll wrap something around it when I get home and it'll be all right in a couple of days.'

'Just what are you doing over there?' Jake asked, suddenly fixing Alex with a penetrating look as if, she thought, he suspected her of some kind of illegal activity. 'I thought the place was coming up for auction next month. In fact, I was thinking of buying it.'

'Oh, were you?' Alex's eyebrows arched in surprise. How her grandfather would have hated that! He had despised the Jensens for the way they put on airs after HP Jensen, Jake's father, had made his millions. 'I came to clean the place up for the auction. But if you're going to buy it, maybe I won't bother. You already owe the Faradays over ten thousand dollars.' She smiled maliciously, then burst out laughing as Jake glared at her.

'Where in hell did you get that idea?' he growled. 'Or are you just joining the legions trying to pry some money from the Jensens?'

'Not at all,' Alex replied calmly. 'My claim is perfectly legitimate. My great-grandfather loaned Carl Jensen a hundred dollars to start his first store, and as far as I can tell it was never paid back. At only five per cent compounded annually, that's over ten thousand by now.'

Jake's eyes had turned to ice. 'Prove it or you won't get a nickel,' he snapped.

Good heavens, he thought she was serious! Alex started to tell him she had been joking, then thought better of it. If he was that sensitive about parting with some of the Jensen millions he deserved to suffer for a while.

'I'm working on it,' she replied. 'I figured you'd be cheap.'

Jake looked as if he were struggling to suppress an impulse to say something loud and ungentlemanly. 'Is there some particular reason why you hate me?' he asked coldly. 'Or is it just men in general you dislike? You haven't said one pleasant word to me since I found you out there.' He lowered Alex's foot to the floor, then leaned back in his chair and stared at her accusingly.

Alex stared back levelly. He really was a very handsome man now, a look of arrogant power replacing the brash boyishness she remembered. With his looks and money he doubtless assumed that every woman within hailing distance was yearning to drop in on him, hoping for some kind of flirtation. She must be annoying him terribly by not behaving in an appropriately worshipful manner! It might be playing with fire, but it would be rather fun to bait him as revenge for all the other poor females who fell at his feet at one glance from those deep blue eyes, only to find their bodies stepped over as the next volunteer appeared. She tilted her head and narrowed her eyes thoughtfully.

'Only you,' she replied to his question. 'First of all, your attitude towards women leaves a great deal to be desired. You assumed that I couldn't possibly know how to fish. I just had to be so interested in seeing you that I'd try any fool trick. As a result, you dumped me into the lake and my boat got wrecked. Also, I now have a sprained ankle, which I really don't need, given all the work I have to do, and which I probably wouldn't have if I'd been left to my own devices. I'm sorry if I seem ill-humoured, but all I really wanted to do this morning was go fishing. Which reminds me, what happened to those fish?' She raised her eyebrows, trying to keep a straight face as Jake Jensen's face reddened, his eyes flashing deep blue distress signals toward her.

'Your damned fish are still in my boat,' he replied, his voice grating with suppressed anger, 'and unfortunately they are apt to be there for a while.' He shifted his gaze to look out at the rain, which was now sliding down the wall of windows in great slithering sheets. 'And I'm afraid you are stuck with my unpleasant company for a while, too, although there's nothing I'd like better than to take you back to your cottage. So——' he stood up abruptly '——I'll see if I can find a bandage for your ankle, and——' his eyes raked her scathingly '——find something dry for you to put on. You are the most bedraggled-looking female I've ever seen.' With that, he turned on his heel and went toward a door beside a large stone fireplace at the back of the room.

'Oh, dear,' Alex murmured, feeling a tightness in her chest at the sight of those massive shoulders disappearing through the door. She had really made Jake mad now. He didn't even want her to stay for dinner any more. Why had she done it? It was as if she couldn't keep herself from taunting him, just as she had years ago. She would have to try to be more pleasant or he'd throw her out in the storm!

Alex took advantage of Jake's absence to look around at her surroundings. The part of the cottage where she was seated was a large, open area. On the left, a slate-topped bar isolated the kitchen and laundry areas, with their attractive beige appliances, from the dining area where she sat, its space defined by a large, round, braided rug. On the other side, surrounding the fireplace, was an arrangement of two large sofas and two big comfortable chairs, a large furry rug between. Near the window wall on that end of the house was a huge desk, situated so that Jake could look out at his dock and the lake beyond when he worked there. The desk was, Alex could see, piled with papers and folders. There was no sign of any servants. It looked very much as if Jake Jensen came here to work and be alone. Maybe even the notorious Jake needed some time off from *amour*!

The minutes ticked by. Where could the man be? Maybe he hoped if he stayed away long enough she'd disappear. She probably did look a fright. Alex felt her hair. Loose ends were stringing from her damp topknot. Charming! Her soggy T-shirt was streaked with some kind of mossy substance from the tree she had climbed. Even her legs had some of it on them. Only her cut-off jeans didn't look much worse than usual, probably because they couldn't. Alex giggled at the image she had of herself, just as Jake Jensen finally reappeared. He looked clean and dry and handsomer than ever in a velour warm-up suit that matched his eyes, but those eyes did not gaze on his giggling guest with any warmth. He merely raised one eyebrow questioningly, a wry look on his face.

'I was thinking how right you must be about how I look,' Alex explained, trying for a friendly smile, but finding herself somewhat unnerved by the blue velvet giant who was staring down at her so intently. 'You couldn't find anything for me to put on? I'm getting kind of cold.'

'I think you should take a bath first. It looks as if you'll be here for a while.' Jake gestured toward the almost night-like sky outside, a brilliant flash of lightning followed quickly by a heavy clap of thunder occurring just as he did so.

'Don't do that!' Alex exclaimed, giggling again at Jake's look of confusion. The remark had come out reflexively, the sort of joke that she and Greg often shared.

'Do what?' Jake asked, frowning.

Alex shook her head. Jake either wasn't very quick on the up-take or he wasn't used to joking around with women, usually having something more basic in mind. 'Never mind,' she said with a sigh.

'Do what?' Jake demanded again. 'Please explain yourself. I don't recall having done anything at all.'

'When you gestured like that——' Alex illustrated with her hand '—it made the lightning flash and the thunder roll. Or are you so used to it that you don't notice any more?' She stared at Jake with wide-eyed innocence, barely able to keep from laughing as he stared back, apparently trying to decide whether she was serious or not. Finally the corners of his mouth quirked a little and she could hold it no longer, bursting into a merry laugh which Jake actually joined.

'I'm sorry I'm so slow today, Alexis,' he apologised when his laughter had died down. 'I guess I should remember to expect the unexpected from you.' He chuckled as Alex made a face at him. 'Now, about that bath. I put a robe in there for you, and I can wash and dry your other things if you want. Ready? Just grab hold.' He bent toward Alex who blinked in surprise.

'Er... why don't you just help me up and let me lean on you? I'm a mess. It'll get your lovely suit all dirty if you carry me.' And she didn't want to give his ego another boost, as well as any other ideas he might have, by playing helpless! The chilly look in his eyes had suddenly turned quite warm again. 'Hey, stop it!' She glared up at Jake, who had swept her up into his arms without any warning.

'You may be ornery, but I am a lot bigger than you,' he pointed out, with a smile that reminded Alex of a boy who has just rung the bell at a carnival to impress his girlfriend. 'I found an elastic bandage you can put on that ankle when you're through, and maybe then you can limp along, but there's no point in making it worse right now.'

'Thank you . . . I think,' Alex said drily.

Jake carried her into the bath, and carefully lowered her to sit on the edge of the tub. 'There,' he said, straightening to his full height and looking down at her like some kind of blue velvet colossus. 'Towels, robe, hair-drier, shampoo, bandages . . .' He pointed to each in turn. 'Anything else you need?'

'That should do it, thanks,' Alex said, feeling rather like Eliza Doolittle being sent off for her first bath. Jake had said she *should* take a bath. 'I'll ring if there's anything else I need,' she added.

'Please do,' Jake replied, pausing by the door to give her a seductive little smile. 'I'll be happy to scrub your back for you.'

Alex turned on a stony look and clapped her hands together. She might try to be pleasant, but Jake Jensen was not going to get any encouragement from her for that kind of nonsense! 'Go!' she said. He did, with a shrug and an unrepentant grin.

Alex winced a little as the steaming water contacted her scrapes, but felt luxurious none the less. The bath, with its mirrored walls, golden fixtures, and thick, sand-coloured carpeting reminded her of a desert oasis. The perfect place for a sheikh to bring his latest conquests!

Apparently, though, none of Jake's women had left a robe behind. The thick white terry robe that Alex put on after her bath was so large she had to turn up the sleeves several times in order to find her hands. She lapped the huge robe across her slender body and tied it tightly with the belt, then gathered her own clothing into a ball and hopped out the door, pausing briefly to peek into the other room which lay at the very back of the earth cottage, deep inside the little hill. It was quite dark, the light from the bathroom behind her only revealing that, as she had thought, it was the bedroom. She alternately hopped and limped back into the main room, her nose picking up the smell of bacon cooking. Food. She hadn't had any breakfast. But was Jake Jensen actually cooking? With one eye she saw that he was, and with the other noticed that Bozo had seen her and was bounding across the floor to welcome her back.

'Whoops! Hello, Bozo,' she said, dropping to her knees to avert being knocked down, her bundle of clothing flying from her hands.

'Oh, there you are. Why in the devil didn't you call me instead of crawling around like that?' Jake came swooping around the end of the bar. He scooped up Alex's clothing and frowned pointedly at her rather utilitarian underwear before tucking the whole mess under his arm. 'Come on, just hold out your arms. I don't have time to argue or the bacon will burn,' he said, crouching before her.

'I was *not* crawling,' Alex grumbled finding herself once again crushed against Jake's hard, muscular chest as he lifted her bodily and carried her to a chair by the table. 'I was hopping along just fine until your dog showed up.' She grinned as Jake cocked a sceptical eyebrow at her before releasing her, then giggled as it suddenly occurred to her what Sarah would think of her present predicament.

'Now what was that about?' Jake asked, giving her a questioning look before hurrying back to his cooking. 'You're awfully thin. I hope you eat regular food, and aren't one of those yo-yos who only eats alfalfa or some such stuff.'

'Alfalfa? Lord, no,' Alex replied, thinking that it was no wonder that Jake thought she might have peculiar eating habits, as strangely as she was behaving. She wasn't usually given to sudden fits of giggling any more than she usually snapped and snarled at people. Jake Jensen certainly didn't bring out the best in her. 'I'm really quite normal,' she said with a sigh. 'I'm just not having a very good day. And then, too,' she added thoughtfully, 'yesterday wasn't a winner either.'

'What happened yesterday?' Jake asked, then added, 'How do you like your eggs?'

'Over easy.' Alex watched, wishing she could see more of this amazing sight—Jake Jensen playing chef. She got up and hopped carefully over to the bar so that she could. 'You're pretty good at that,' she said, as he deftly broke eggs into a frying pan.

'Apparently I'm not supposed to be,' he retorted, casting a quick glance back at her. 'Or is it just that men aren't supposed to be in the kitchen?'

'Touché,' Alex said. 'I'm kind of surprised, though, that you don't have someone around to keep house and cook for you.'

'I get tired of having people around. Any people.' He glanced at Alex. 'Although I did think I might find your company interesting for a while.'

'And now you're not so sure?' Alex shrugged. 'I don't blame you.' If she had come here to be alone she certainly wouldn't welcome someone who had been as much of a nuisance as she had.

At that Jake looked over at Alex and smiled warmly. 'I haven't thrown you out yet, have I?' he said, as he began to carry things to the table. 'OK, let's hop on back,' he said finally, coming to take Alex's arm.

She accompanied him silently, feeling suddenly that she wished she hadn't intruded upon his solitude. But then, she wouldn't have if he hadn't come along to 'help' her.

'Everything all right, or are you still brooding about whatever went wrong yesterday?' he asked as she fell to eating, feeling a strange disquietude at being here, alone, with this powerful man who made her react so strangely.

'Oh, no, everything's fine,' she replied, looking up to see him watching her intently. 'I'm sorry, I was just thinking. I guess this storm's got my nerves on edge. I wish it would stop so I could go home. Poor Murphy's probably climbing the walls.'

'Murphy?'

'My cat. He hates storms.'

'He'll be all right.' There was an almost comforting quality to Jake's deep voice. 'Want to tell me about yesterday, or is it a secret? A broken romance?'

Alex glanced briefly into that intense blue gaze and then looked down and shook her head. Jake *would* think of that. 'Neither,' she replied. 'I just...became unemployed.' She had been going to say more, but suddenly felt it wasn't something she wanted to tell Jake Jensen. He might be decidedly lacking in sympathy, given his reputation for not promoting women at Jenstar.

'Mmmm. That's too bad,' Jake said sympathetically. 'What do you do? We have openings at Jenstar for all kinds of people.'

'Well, I wouldn't...' Alex caught herself, blushing as Jake's eyes narrowed, as if he could read her mind. What was wrong with her? She had just been stupidly going to say that she wouldn't work for Jenstar on a bet! And here was Jake, only trying to be nice and helpful to someone whom he probably thought was only a poor little clerk who'd been fired from some menial job. 'I wouldn't want to trouble you,' she finished lamely. 'I don't think Jenstar would be interested in me.'

Jake leaned back in his chair and looked at Alex thoughtfully. 'Strange,' he said. 'First I meet a very aggressive woman, and now all of a sudden you're a shrinking violet, who seems embarrassed about something. That must mean that someone had the bad judgement to fire you. Or did you deserve it?' he added as Alex glanced at him sharply.

'I don't want to discuss it,' she said coldly, wondering why he insisted on pursuing the topic. If he didn't stop it . . .

'Alex, if there is one thing I'm an expert on, it's employee problems,' Jake said, slathering jam on a piece of toast. 'You might as well take advantage of it and tell me your story.'

All right, you asked for it, Alex thought grimly, feeling her nerves tightening dangerously. She lifted her chin and looked Jake straight in the eyes. 'I wasn't fired, I resigned,' she said. 'I was in line to become Vice President for Economic Forecasting at the Northern Grain Consortium in Minneapolis. They chose to give the job to a totally incompetent male instead. I fought their blasted sex discrimination for three years, but that was the last straw. So you can see why Jenstar wouldn't be interested in me, and I wouldn't be interested in Jenstar.'

Oh, boy, I've done it now, she thought, feeling her hands actually tremble as Jake set his fork down with a clatter, a black scowl drawing his brows almost together. His voice was only slightly below the roar of the thunder as he said, 'I resent your implications! Jenstar always has and will continue to deal fairly with women!'

'Then you'd better get someone to improve your public image,' Alex responded with a fairly loud roar of her own, clutching her fork tightly and willing herself not to flinch beneath Jake's ferocious glare. 'I've seen articles which said differently, and I also saw a decidedly unfortunate quote of yours. You'll have scared off any woman with any sense by now.'

'I doubt it,' Jake retorted. 'Anyone with any sense knows better than to believe everything they read in the papers.' He tilted his head and eyed Alex critically. 'What makes you so sure you were discriminated against? I've heard the same story plenty of times before, and when I looked into it it didn't hold water.'

'You're welcome to look into this one,' Alex snapped back. 'The relative competence is there in black and white for anyone to see. If I were a male with a family to support I'd have been a dead cert.' She smiled suddenly. 'I'd love to go back in six months and see what kind of a disaster that idiot Noel Smith has created. He doesn't know demographics from geographics.'

Now what's on his mind? Alex wondered, as Jake's frown suddenly cleared and flickering lights appeared in his eyes, which narrowed as he stared at her. However, he said nothing, merely making a 'hmmm' sort of sound before going back to his breakfast. Well, at least he hadn't thrown anything at her...yet. 'Why don't you let me do that?' she suggested, thinking perhaps she'd better try to be helpful, as Jake, still silent, got up and started removing the dirty dishes from the table. 'If I just had something to use for a cane, I could manage.'

'Thanks, but it will only take a minute,' he replied, giving Alex a quick little smile. 'I'm pretty good at doing dishes, too.'

'Amazing,' she said drily, feeling a rush of relief that his good humour had apparently returned. 'Well, if you won't accept my help I'll just hop on over to another chair and read until the storm lets up. Just pretend I'm not here.'

'Do I have to?' Jake paused beside her, and Alex was suddenly terribly aware of the breadth of his shoulders and the intense blue of his thick-lashed eyes.

'No, of course not,' she replied, grimacing as she put her weight on her sore ankle to try to maintain an equilibrium that all at once felt wobbly. What did she care whether he pretended or not?

'Good. Then come and tell me about your work while I clean up. Here, lean on me. I can tell that ankle hurts.' He helped Alex on to one of the cushioned stools and then went around to the other side of the bar. 'How long were you at Northern Grain?'

'Almost four years. Trying to find out if I'm competent?' Alex asked, leaning her chin on her hand and watching as Jake began filling the sink with water.

'Exactly,' Jake replied.

'Why? You can't get me that promotion.'

Jake paused in his work and leaned across the counter, his face only inches from Alex. 'I can get you something better,' he said, smiling and giving a light tap to the tip of her nose with his finger. 'I may have the perfect job for you at Jenstar.'

CHAPTER THREE

'Here. Read this.' Jake tossed a bound report on to Alex's lap. 'It's a preliminary report from the former Head of Economic Forecasting at Jenstar,' he added as Alex looked at him questioningly. 'See if you can figure out why he's no longer with us. I have some paperwork to do for a couple of hours. That should keep you busy.'

'OK,' Alex said, puzzled. Jake had asked her a lot of questions, but surely he couldn't be thinking of her in terms of replacing the former Head of Economic Forecasting at Jenstar! No, of course not. He probably had some other position in that department to fill. Oh, well. It could still be a step up from where she'd been at Northern Grain. She opened the report and was soon absorbed so completely that when Jake said, near her ear, 'Get anything out of that report?' her head jerked up with a start.

'Don't sneak up like that,' she said crossly. She had been concentrating so hard she hadn't heard his footsteps.

Jake grinned. 'Sorry. Well, did you?' He sank down on the couch beside her.

'Of course I did,' Alex snapped, flipping through the pages. 'This part on Peach Records as a possible acquisition to expand Jenstar into the entertainment field is a disaster. Some of the data are contradictory, several factors that were used on similar evaluations were left out, and there's nothing about the management, or any comparisons with other companies, either. I can't imagine why, on the basis of what's here, the conclusion was positive.'

'You found it!' Jake cried triumphantly, with such force that Alex stared at him in wide-eyed surprise. 'By God, you found it!'

'It wasn't quite as hard as finding the Holy Grail,' Alex said drily. 'Any reasonably competent person could have done it. Or are you just surprised because I'm a woman?'

'Sex has nothing to do with it,' Jake snapped, his pleasant expression changing to one of aggravation. 'In case you hadn't noticed, the world is not overstocked with competent people of either sex, and, contrary to any nonsense you've read, I am perfectly capable of recognising them when I see them, without regard to gender.'

Alex raised her eyebrows sceptically. 'I still find it hard to believe that you haven't found even one to move into top management at Jenstar.'

This time Jake's lips disappeared completely and he made a snorting sound. For a few moments he stared at Alex as if contemplating saying something very uncomplimentary. Finally he let out a breath, his eyes flashing in annoyance.

'You are the most aggravating, over-confident, back-talking female I've ever met,' he growled. 'God only knows why I want to make you the first woman executive at Jenstar, but I do, and I want you to start next week, as chief of our Economic Forecasting division.'

Next week? She could have *that* job and he wanted her to start next week? 'But...I don't know if I want that job.' Alex stared at Jake Jensen, open-mouthed, dizzily wondering if she were dreaming or only losing her mind.

'Of course you do. You'd be crazy not to,' Jake said, getting to his feet. He looked down at Alex with a maddeningly confident smile. 'Close your mouth. You look like a fish. Which reminds me——' he looked out through the wall of glass '—it's not raining quite as hard. I'll try to rescue those bass for dinner. If you don't mind sharing them.'

'No...I'd be...happy to,' Alex said, still in a daze. Her eyes followed Jake as he grabbed a rain poncho from a hook and put it on, muttered a 'Damn it, Bozo, stay in', and slipped out the door. She stood and watched, feeling as if a strange, almost umbilical connection had formed between her and the tall man who ran, hunched against the wind, to the boat. She found herself holding her breath until he had picked up the fish, and run back, the wind whipping the heavy poncho about him as if it were tissue paper. How had he done it? She had not come here looking for either him or the Jenstar job. And now, with a few terse sentences, he seemed to think he had taken over her life! Well, he could just back off a little bit and give her some time to think. Crazy or not, she wasn't sure she wanted that job...

'Phew,' Jake said, pushing the poncho hood back as he re-entered the cottage and shaking his head, water flying from his black hair. 'This is the worst storm we've had here in quite a while.'

'They don't usually last this long.' Alex hobbled over to stare out at the wind-swept lake, huge white-caps rolling across its surface beneath a sky that still looked heavy as lead. The world outside looked as roiled as she felt, and there was still no sign of its letting up. 'Poor Murphy,' she said, suddenly remembering her staunch little friend. 'He's going to think I've abandoned him, all alone in this strange, terrible place. I hope he's finding a lot of mice to entertain him.'

'You really love that cat, don't you?' Jake commented from the kitchen, where he was beginning to operate on the fish. 'Think he'll like living in New York?'

'He wouldn't mind. He's an indoor cat,' Alex replied. She limped over to sit on a bar stool and watch Jake proficiently skinning the bass with hands that looked too big for such delicate precision. 'I haven't said I'd take the job yet, though.'

Jake raised his eyebrows and gave her a knowing look. 'You will. You can't resist it.'

Alex made a face. 'You seem to think you can read my mind. I don't think I like that.'

'On the contrary.' Jake leaned close to the counter and looked directly into Alex's eyes. 'You find it fascinating.'

Did she? Alex wondered, averting her gaze after a moment. It was certainly different. She wished she were having better luck reading Jake's. That knowing little smile had a certain warmth to it that hadn't been there earlier. She could almost feel the warmth on her skin, and it made her tingle strangely. He had better not be getting any ideas about mixing business with pleasure.

'*If* I take the job,' she said primly, 'it certainly can't be next week. I have to get the Faraday cottage ready for the auction, and then I'd have to go home and sublet my apartment. Besides, I didn't come to Tamarack looking for a job, I came for a vacation. I haven't had one in years.'

Jake smiled knowingly. 'You'd rather have the job than an indefinitely long vacation, wouldn't you?'

Hmmm, Alex thought suspiciously. There had to be some reason he was trying to push her into making such a quick decision. Was it just his typically macho attempt to gain the upper hand, or were the women's groups beginning to put some uncomfortable pressure on him?

'I'm not so sure,' she replied coolly. 'What woman in her right mind wants to work for a man who thinks there is only one position suitable for a woman?' She knew she had struck a nerve when Jake pounded his fist down on the cutting block so hard that the fish jumped into the air.

'That remark had nothing to do with Jenstar or with business at all!' he roared. 'I don't want to hear any more about that from you or anyone else. Maybe some day I'll tell you what it was really about, but in the meantime, lay off of that topic or you'll find yourself unemployed before you're even employed!'

'Wouldn't it be simpler,' Alex said, ignoring his dictum, 'if you'd just explain it to me and the rest of the world now?'

Jake looked as if he would like to take the filleting knife to Alex as he glared at her. 'No, it would not. It involves a situation that is very complicated, very unpleasant, and very, very sticky. That is all I am going to say on the subject, and it is for your ears only. Do you understand?'

'Of course,' Alex replied. And it also made her very, very curious, she thought. It sounded as if he might have got himself into a really tricky situation, probably with some woman. She would have to keep her ear to the ground when she got to Jenstar. Hmmm...*when* she got to Jenstar? Did that mean she had decided to take the job? She smiled wryly to herself. Jake was probably right that she couldn't resist it, but she wasn't going to tell him so yet.

'What was that little smirk about?' Jake asked, seeing her smile. 'Think you have it all figured out?'

Alex raised her eyebrows. 'Why ask? I thought you could read my mind.'

Jake grinned but did not reply. 'There,' he said, as he laid the neat fillets out side by side, 'ready to cook. It's almost six o'clock. Want to help get dinner?'

'Sure,' Alex said, glad of a chance to do something besides sit and stare at Jake Jensen. She slid off the stool, wrenching at the robe, which tangled about her legs. 'I could do better if I weren't trapped like a mummy in this robe,' she complained. 'Why do you have to be so big?'

Jake laughed outright at that. 'Sorry. I can't help it, but this will. I got your clothes clean again while you were reading.' He held out the neatly folded little pile to her. 'You're going to have to do something about your underwear. That bra looks like something you'd wear to Girl Guide camp.'

'You never mind about my underwear! That bra is for jogging.' Alex snatched the pile from his hand and clutched it to her. 'Besides that, it's none of your business!' Drat the man! She could actually feel her cheeks growing warm in embarrassment.

'I'm always interested in ladies' underwear,' Jake said easily, grinning broadly at Alex's discomfort. 'In case you hadn't noticed, Jenstar owns one of the largest manufacturers of women's undergarments, Princess Lydia. I like to picture the women I meet wearing some of our nicer products.'

'Well, while you're playing your little chauvinistic games, you can just picture me in an old-fashioned red union suit,' Alex said coldly. 'Better yet, just stop them all together or I won't take the job.'

Jake shook his head, a completely unrepentant twinkle in his eyes. 'I don't think you're all that upset. In fact, I think you're delighted to have a man interested in your underwear.' He narrowed his eyes thoughtfully. 'I was thinking more along the lines of something pale blue with a lot of lace. Mostly lace, I think.'

'Will you just drop it!' Alex could almost feel his eyes penetrating through the thick robe as he looked her up and down. It was giving her the chills! 'How would you like it if I started speculating about your underwear?' She turned scarlet as Jake roared with laughter. 'Oh, God, I knew as soon as I opened my mouth I was putting my foot in it,' she muttered, dropping her head forward and rubbing her forehead. 'Look,' she said pleadingly, trying to regain her composure, 'I just want to have dinner and get home and see my cat. When is it going to stop raining? Can't you take me anyway?'

'I'm afraid Murphy might end up an orphan. The wind is still gusting up to about forty miles an hour out there. I listened to the radio a while ago, and as near as I could tell through the static they said it should be all clear by morning.'

'Morning!' Alexis cried. 'I can't stay here all night!' What would poor Murphy do? What might Jake Jensen, with his new interest in her underwear, do? She wasn't sure she could trust him. That funny way he was smiling at her now looked very much like Murphy when he sat on the windowsill, watching the birds outside.

'I'm afraid you'll just have to live with it, Alex,' Jake said calmly. 'Now run along and change. Working on dinner will help get your mind off of your troubles.'

'Run along?' Alex said sarcastically as she hobbled off in the direction of the bathroom. He needn't treat her like an idiot child just because she was worried about her cat. She went into the bathroom and locked the door, avoiding looking in the huge mirror as she put on her plain white nylon bra and panties. There was nothing wrong with them. Nothing at all. She liked things simple. What was so terrible about that?

'What can I do to help?' she asked when she returned to the kitchen, feeling much more mobile now that she was out of the clutches of Jake's huge robe.

'See what you can find in the fridge to make some salad,' Jake suggested. 'It's a good thing you caught these fish. I wasn't expecting company.'

'I wasn't expecting to *be* company,' Alex replied, peering into the refrigerator and retrieving a head of lettuce, a tomato, and a cucumber. 'Where do I find a bowl?'

'Up there.' Jake gestured to a cupboard.

Alex found the bowl and then looked around for a place to put it down. Between Jake's size and the way he had his fish-frying project spread out, there wasn't much room. 'Can you consolidate your fish a little more?' she suggested.

'Sure,' Jake said agreeably, sliding some of his utensils out of the way and giving Alex another of those warm smiles.

Is there something I'm missing? Alex wondered, feeling a little ripple of confusion that temporarily disorientated her. 'Excuse me,' she said, shaking her head to try to clear it. She bumped into Jake as she moved to wash the lettuce, and found it rather like running into a warm, velvet-covered tree. 'I don't think your architect designed this kitchen for someone your size,' she commented, looking up at him and then looking quickly back at her head of lettuce, pretending that it fascinated her. There was that smile again! It made her feel prickly all over.

'I'm afraid standard kitchen equipment is still designed for women,' Jake agreed. 'Maybe we should start a line for men.'

'I don't think the world's ready for that yet,' Alex said. 'I think most men would rather you manufactured a robot that looked like a woman that they could put in a regular kitchen.'

Jake chuckled. 'Probably so. Am I safe in assuming that you don't have any plans for being the robot in someone's kitchen? That is, there's no man in Minneapolis that makes you reluctant to leave right away?'

Alex gave him a sideways glance. Why did he assume that? She wasn't that bad looking! 'You aren't supposed to ask prospective employees things like that,' she said. 'If I take the job I will do the job. A man, if there is one, will not interfere.'

'It was a purely personal question. I asked because I want to know. Is there a man in your life?' Jake repeated.

Alex turned from slicing the tomato, frowning. Jake certainly wasn't short on tenacity when he got on to a line of questioning. Well, it wasn't any of his business that she hadn't had any men in her life lately. 'No comment,' she said coldly.

Jake was bent over the frying fish, shaking salt on to the crusty brown side that was now on the top. He wheeled, still bent, so that his face was level with Alex's and only inches away. 'Alex,' he said softly, his eyes glittering strangely, 'answer me. I know about your underwear and now I want to know about your love-life...or lack of it.'

Alex glared at him. Why did he insist on peeling his way into the very core of her life as if she were no more than an onion on his chopping block? Suddenly she was aware of the irresistible combination of Jake's face so close and the tomato in her right hand. 'That is none of your business,' she said, simultaneously smashing the soft tomato against his nose. 'And you can keep your blasted job,' she added, thinking grimly, as Jake's eyes grew almost black with fury, that it probably wasn't open to her any longer, anyway.

He wiped the tomato off with a hastily grabbed towel, still fixing her with a look that could have peeled paint from a building, but saying nothing. He was, Alex thought, building up a fearful head of steam.

'Tend the fish before they burn,' she suggested, turning back to her salad preparations, wondering when the blast was going to hit. The seconds ticked by and nothing happened. Alex could feel her stomach churning. Why had she done it? It had been tempting, but good lord! She wasn't still fourteen! She heard the sound of a plate being taken from a cupboard, of the fish being removed from the pan. She had finished cutting up the salad ingredients, but she was afraid to turn around and look at Jake, lest that was the cue he was waiting for to fire his salvo. He moved closer, stopping right beside her. She waited, not moving.

'Miss Faraday...' the soft voice came so close to her ear that she could feel his breath '... are you always so obnoxious?'

'Always,' Alex replied. She turned her head only slightly, but her cheek bumped against his chin and she startled at the shock of its roughness. 'Are you?' There was no point in retreating now.

'Yes. Miss Faraday?'

'What?' Here it comes.

'Am I right in assuming that your violent response indicates a bitter affair in your past?'

'No!' And I wouldn't tell you if there was.

'Then why haven't you married? Why no man in your life? I'm right in assuming there isn't one, aren't I?'

Good lord, what tenacity! 'There have been plenty of men, but no one special!' Alex almost shouted in Jake's ear. 'I've been too busy. Look, I'm not prying into your personal life. You can take every woman in North America to bed for all I care.'

Jake made a growling sound. 'The media grossly exaggerate my exploits. If they were half of what I've been credited with I would have dropped from exhaustion years ago. As someone with your background ought to know, I, too, have been damned busy. One other thing, Miss Faraday.'

'Now what?' Maybe this time?

'About that blasted job. I've decided I don't want you in New York in a week.'

'I didn't think you would.'

'I want you there on Friday.'

'You what?' Alex turned toward Jake so swiftly that he had to set the plate of fish down hurriedly and catch her as her ankle gave way. 'Are you some kind of masochist?' she asked, amazed, as he smiled at her, supporting her with one arm around her while he toyed with a lock of her hair with the other hand. Did he actually like having tomatoes in the face? If he did, he was certainly one of the most mixed-up men she'd ever met. 'Why,' she persisted, 'does that make you want me to come to New York on Friday? Stop that.'

She took his hand and removed it from her hair, frowning, which only made his smile grow broader, some kind of changing lights making his blue eyes appear deep enough to plunge into and...drown?

'Masochist? Not me,' he replied, still smiling. 'I admire someone who slings tomatoes on principle, when it could cost them their job.'

'Oh,' Alex said, still feeling confused. If only he'd stop smiling like that. She tried to get back to the topic at hand.

'I really don't understand what kind of game you're playing, Jake. If I decide to take the job, I will take care of my business in Minneapolis as quickly as humanly possible and then go to New York. You can just stop this next week and Friday stuff.'

'I only want to pin you down to a schedule, so you'll be less likely to tell me you'll take the job and then change your mind,' Jake said. 'It's important I get someone in that position as soon as possible. The report on Peach Records has to be done over before the board meeting on the first of next month, or...my option with the owner may not be renewed.'

'Well, why didn't you say so in the first place?' Alex asked, frowning. Still, she wanted some time to think it over. 'I'll let you know in the morning. My mother told me to always sleep on important decisions. Now let's eat those fish before they get cold.'

'Far be it from me to undermine a mother's training,' Jake said drily, picking up the platter and heading for the table.

'Hah!' Alex commented, following him with the salad. She would be willing to bet that the world was filled with mothers who would be appalled to know how thoroughly Jake Jensen had undermined their best efforts. He was only safe when his mind was on business, and that was where she would keep it. 'How about answering a few questions about Jenstar?' she suggested as she took her place at the table. 'Now that I've done some reading, I've got a couple of hundred.'

'Enough!' Jake said finally, when Alex had pursued her tactic through dinner, the dishes, and another couple of hours. 'Let's get some sleep so we can greet the sun that's supposed to appear in the morning.'

'Good idea,' Alex agreed, stifling a yawn. 'Just find me a blanket and I'll curl up on the couch.'

'That wouldn't be very hospitable of me,' Jake said, shaking his head. 'You take the bed and give those banged-up bones of yours a good rest. Come on now, don't argue,' he added, as Alex started to protest. 'I've never had a woman here to appreciate my beautiful bedroom.'

Alex made a sceptical face at that statement but said nothing, reluctantly limping after him. Her eyes grew wide and her mouth formed a silent 'Oh' as he flipped on the lights. There were massive floral prints on the walls and on the quilted cover on the king-size bed. The carpet was a deep, soft green. Rather than looking like a gloomy room, buried in a hillside, with no windows at all, the effect was of being in a garden.

'It *is* beautiful,' she said, smiling up at Jake. 'It looks like a Gauguin painting.'

'That was what I tried for,' he admitted, his pleasure at her response lighting his face. 'Of course, I had to have a decorator carry it out. I don't know about such things as fabrics and carpets.'

'It was a marvellous plan,' said Alex. Somehow she would never have suspected Jake of having an artistic streak, but he obviously did, and a very talented one.

'I think you could have a whole new career if you wanted it.'

'Thank you, ma'am,' Jake said, seeming almost embarrassed at her praise. He went to the dresser. 'You could sleep in this,' he suggested, handing a pyjama top to Alex. 'I only use the bottoms myself.'

'All right,' Alex agreed, trying to ignore the disturbingly intimate thoughts that sprang to mind at the idea of them sharing one set of pyjamas. 'Are you sure you'll be comfortable on the couch?' she asked doubtfully, looking at the huge bed he was used to and then back at his towering height.

'Perfectly,' he assured her. He got a blanket from the wardrobe and started for the door. 'Do you want me to tuck you in?' he asked with a teasing grin, as Alex still stood by the bed, the pyjama top in her hand.

'Of course not,' she said tightly, feeling more than a little uncomfortable, but not sure exactly why. 'I'm just waiting for you to leave.'

'Goodnight, then,' Jake said. 'Sleep well.' He gave Alex another of those warm little smiles.

'You...you, too. Goodnight.'

As the door clicked shut behind him, Alex looked at the silky blue pyjama top and frowned. Somehow she felt safer fully clothed. But that was silly. She shouldn't let Jake unnerve her like that. Flirting with women was as natural to him as breathing, and it didn't mean a thing. How many foolish women must have thought there was really a message in that entrancing smile of his? She took off her clothes and laid them on a chair, then slipped on the pyjama top. Her eyes fell again on her discarded clothing. 'Damn,' she muttered. He had certainly made her aware of her underwear. She could hardly bear to

look at it! With a swift move, she tucked it beneath her
shirt and shorts. 'There. Now you can't stare at me,' she
said grimly, making doubly sure by quickly climbing into
bed and turning off the light.

CHAPTER FOUR

ALEX awoke with a start during the night, and stared around the darkened room, trying to sort out where she was and why she was awake in the middle of the night, finally deciding that it was the throbbing of her ankle that had awakened her. Maybe Jake had some aspirin somewhere in that elaborate bathroom. She would have a look.

'Bzzzz...Nasush maad...Mmmmm...OK...Bzzzz.'

The strange string of sounds came from Alex's left. She turned her head slowly, her pulse beginning to quicken. Could it be what it sounded like? A man...snoring and mumbling in his sleep? It could! There, only a couple of feet away, was a black head on the next pillow! The colossal nerve of the man! With a violent motion, Alex thrust herself toward the edge of the bed.

'You creep!' she cried, hitting the floor with a thud and tugging the pyjama top down simultaneously.

The inert figure on the bed began to thrash about and then sat up.

'What's wrong?' demanded a growly voice.

'What's wrong?' Alex squeaked incredulously. *'You're* what's wrong! How dare you sneak into bed with me? I should have known a man with your reputation would try something like that. What does a woman have to do to discourage...'

'Oh, for God's sake, Alexis, shut up,' Jake grated, snapping on the bedside light and glowering at her darkly. He rubbed his eyes. 'I found out the sofa bothered my back. I hurt it skiing last winter. It didn't seem to me it would do any harm for me to sleep in here. The bed's big enough for two.'

'Not with me in it, it isn't,' Alex snapped back. She picked up her pile of clothing. 'I'll go and sleep on the sofa. Where are you going?' Jake had got out of bed and was moving toward her, his bare chest with its V of black curls looming as large as a grizzly bear, the black stubble on his chin lending a menacing cast to his disgusted expression.

'To get a drink, if you don't mind,' he replied, raising one eyebrow and twisting his mouth in a sarcastic smile. 'You needn't labour under the misapprehension that I'm trying to seduce you. If I were, you'd know it...' He stopped in front of her and raked her up and down with his eyes '...and I doubt if you'd complain.' Somehow, as his eyes swept from Alex's tousled hair, down her long, shapely legs, and back to meet her flashing eyes, his smile changed to a warmly seductive one.

'Don't bet on it,' Alex said coldly, shivering at that practised look which doubtless unhinged many a normally stable female. The man could practically do it in his sleep!

Jake's smile edged up a little on one side and his eyes twinkled. 'For such a liberated woman, you seem to have quite a prudish streak.'

'I am not a prude,' Alex denied. 'However, I don't see any reason why being liberated in the boardroom means you have to be liberated in the bedroom, too. Oh! Stop it!' she cried, her words becoming muffled as Jake suddenly grabbed her, tucked one hand behind her head, and covered her mouth with his.

Alex tried to wrench herself free, but Jake was too strong, and having only one good leg to stand on made her efforts even less effective. When twisting back and forth did no good she changed her tactics to standing motionless, trying to ignore the sensations of solidity and warmth that emanated from the body against which her own scantily clad body was so tightly held, and the softness of the lips that pressed against hers. I won't respond, I won't! she promised herself, trying to still the racing pulse she could feel pounding in her throat as those lips made softly sucking sorties across her mouth, and the tip of Jake's tongue tickled at the corners of her closed lips, sending a wave of panic racing through her like a shot of adrenalin. Good lord! She felt as if she were on fire! Jake had laced his fingertips through her hair, and their action on her scalp and behind her ears was mesmerising. Her skin felt as if it had taken on a life of its own, responding with flaring excitement to the pressure of Jake's body. Her breasts could feel the roughness of his chest through the thin silk of her pyjama top, betraying an ever-increasing desire to rub against it, and sending signals of other, deeper yearnings. The total effect was as dizzying as a carnival ride, terrifying and yet exciting, and impossible to stop. With a tiny groan, Alex abandoned her efforts to resist, her swollen lips answering the demands of Jake's persistent assault. Her bundle of clothing fell to the floor as her arms went around him, her hands clutching at the smooth skin of his broad, muscular back. She could feel his answering arousal as her response became more reckless, her fingernails digging into his back with the eagerness of her desire to press even closer.

With one hand, Jake pulled up the back of Alex's pyjama top and then smoothed gently across her bare bottom.

'Ouch' Alex cried, jerking backwards. Suddenly she had been pinched—quite firmly. She stared up into Jake's laughing eyes, feeling a flush rush to her cheeks. 'What do you think you're doing?' she demanded, his sudden switch leaving her suspended, like a rider stuck at the top of a ferris wheel.

'Just verifying that I was right. You didn't complain...and, as I thought, you are a very passionate woman. With very sharp fingernails.' He chuckled as Alex backed away, scowling.

She glared at him. 'I didn't have a chance to complain, but I'm doing it now. I wish my fingernails were twice as sharp. You're a...a...' Alex could not think of any word that seemed right, her mind still reeling at the wild response that Jake Jensen had elicited from her. She had never before felt so overpowered by a man. She did not like it. She did not like it at all! She was definitely not going to let that happen again!

'A rotten bastard?' Jake offered helpfully, still grinning.

'That's putting it mildly! And if that wasn't sexual harassment of the worst kind...'

'You're not my employee yet,' Jake said calmly, 'so don't start accusing me. But...' he bent and picked up Alex's clothing and handed the pile to her '...if you want to prevent any future episodes like that, after you are, don't bait me.' He lifted one eyebrow, his eyes twinkling devilishly. 'I don't think it's sexual harassment when both parties want it.'

'Don't flatter yourself!' Alex replied, ignoring his laughter as she turned and stalked angrily toward the living-room with as much dignity as she could muster on her bad ankle, trying frantically to remember just what she had done to precipitate Jake's assault and finding it impossible. She had no sooner passed through the doorway by the fireplace when all thoughts on that topic were erased by the beautiful sight before her.

'Oh, Jake, look,' she breathed, hobbling to look out the windows where, bathed in moonlight almost as bright as day, the lake shimmered and sparkled.

'Magnificent, isn't it?' Jake said, coming to stand beside her. 'I've always loved watching the lake by moonlight.' He put his arm lightly around Alex's shoulders. 'It looks almost unreal, like a magical world where things can happen that never really do by day. It's never like this in the city.'

There was a husky, almost sad note in Jake's voice that made Alex glance up at him quickly. Just as quickly she looked away again. He was looking at her so strangely! What kind of game was he playing now? Suddenly painfully aware of him again, of the arm on her shoulders, she held still, scarcely breathing, feeling terribly vulnerable.

'I know,' she said softly. 'Sometimes I wish I'd taken up an occupation that let me live in a place like this and take my vacations in the city, instead of the other way around.'

'Me, too,' Jake said, giving her shoulders a little squeeze.

Alex glanced up at him again. He was looking out toward the lake now, the angular planes of his face deeply etched by the moonlight. A warm wave of dizziness swept over her as she stared at him, entranced. Oh, no! she thought, as a chill of fear replaced the warmth. She was reacting just like any silly woman! Just like Sarah! This had to stop! 'You . . . you could take me home now,' she suggested haltingly. 'There's scarcely any wind.'

'Not a chance.' Jake's reply was gruff, his hand quickly withdrawn. 'I'm still hoping to get some sleep tonight. So far I haven't had much luck!' With that he walked swiftly toward the bar, found a bottle of brandy and poured himself a generous shot. 'Want some?' he asked, holding the bottle up toward Alex, who was moving slowly toward the sofa, trying to get her wildly fluctuating emotions under control.

'No, thanks,' she replied. 'I'm having enough trouble walking stone-cold sober.' And enough trouble coping with you, too, she added to herself. No wonder Jake's reputation was as torrid as it was! He must know every way under the sun to weaken a woman's resistance. She was going to have to learn some counter measures, very fast!

It was Alex who had trouble sleeping the rest of the night, tossing and turning and punching viciously at her pillow. Should she take the job with Jenstar, or was she letting herself in for more trouble than she could handle? The job itself was daunting, far more complex than anything she had done before. Still, she was sure she could handle it if Jake gave her the time . . . and space . . . to do it. But if he hovered over her and insisted on playing sexual games . . . Well, she'd have to make it clear that she wouldn't put up with that! It could be the opportunity of a lifetime, and if she couldn't cope it was as much as admitting that any woman couldn't. She couldn't let the whole sex down now. Where there was a will, there had to be a way.

It seemed to Alex that she had just fallen asleep when Jake, looking bright and chipper, told her it was time to rise and shine.

'Get dressed. I'll have breakfast ready in a jiffy and then I'll take you back to your lonesome kitty cat.'

'Oh, poor Murphy!' In her confusion, Alex had almost forgotten her furry friend. She got quickly out of her temporary bed, gathered up her clothing and headed toward the bath.

'Here. You're leaving a trail.'

Alex stopped and turned just in time to receive the bra which Jake held out toward her with an evil twinkle in his eyes. 'Thank you,' she said stiffly, swivelling quickly away to hide the blush which came to her cheeks. You idiot! she scolded herself. She couldn't remember having blushed so much in years! She rushed into the bathroom and took a quick shower, trying to get her sleepy mind to function properly. It was not a great success. She still felt as if her head were filled with something as scrambled as the eggs which Jake served her when she returned to the dining-table. When he asked, 'Well, what's the verdict?' she stared at him blankly.

'About what? Oh, the eggs are fine,' she finally replied.

Jake shook his head and sighed. 'I meant about the job,' he said.

'Oh, that!' Alex exclaimed, then flushed with embarrassment as Jake roared with laughter. 'I'm not awake yet,' she said testily. 'Yes, I'll take it. If you'll agree not to make any more passes at me, and treat me exactly as you would any male employee.' She tried to fix Jake with a serious look, but found it difficult in the face of his amused smile. 'I must say you're not exactly getting off on the right foot now,' she added coldly.

'Sorry,' Jake replied, without any visible signs of contrition. 'All right, I agree. I shall do my best, as long as you behave exactly like any male employee. Fair enough?'

'Certainly,' Alex agreed. At least, she hoped it was.

It was less than an hour later that they were on their way back to the Faraday cottage, Alex in front with Jake this time, and Bozo taking command of the rear seat.

'There isn't a dock at my place any more,' Alex shouted to Jake as he took off from his dock with a deafening roar of the powerful engine and flashed around the end of the island in what, she assumed, was the only way he knew to drive the blasted boat, 'so you can just let me jump out and wade in. I'll drive into town right away and locate someone to finish the cleaning, and I should be able to start for Minneapolis by tomorrow morning. If you're going to be back in New York on Wednesday I can call you to let you know when I can be there.'

'Why can't you leave for Minneapolis later today?' Jake shouted back, an imperious note in his voice as if, Alex thought grimly, he was ready to take command of her life as well as her occupation.

'Because I have to finish going through the family keepsakes,' she yelled. 'A chore which I would have finished long ago if that dreadful storm hadn't come up. Which reminds me, it was an old book I found that told about that loan...' more softly, as Jake slowed the motor to an idle, letting the boat drift slowly toward the shore, and turned to look at her. 'It's a combination of ledger and diary, with all kinds of interesting things about the price of mules and who married who, and how they kept someone's body in the ice shed until spring when the ground thawed enough to dig a grave.'

Jake chuckled. 'That book does sound interesting,' he said. 'I know my father would like to see it, too. Why don't you bring it with you to New York? He should be back in New York soon for the directors' meeting.'

'I didn't realise he was still active in the corporation,' Alex said, surprised. The story Tamarack residents told was that HP Jensen had retired when Jake's mother had died, so heartbroken that he had suffered a nervous breakdown. 'I'm glad to hear he's recovered from the loss of your mother.'

'Oh, he's recovered all right,' Jake said drily. 'He spends his winters in Beverly Hills mingling with the movie people and his summers in New York, driving me crazy. In fact, I'd better warn you about him. He never hesitates to make a pass at a pretty girl. On second thoughts...' Jake grinned suddenly as Alex frowned '...I'd better warn him about you.'

'Do that,' Alex said with a firm nod. All she needed was another lecherous Jensen to make her life complete!

There was a scraping noise as the big boat touched the lake bottom, and Alex stood up and flung her legs over the side of the boat, then lowered herself into the thigh-deep water.

'Hand me my tackle box, will you, please?' she said, holding out her hand.

'Sure thing,' Jake replied, handing her the box. 'I guess this is goodbye for now.' He gave Alex an extra-warm smile.

'Yes, I guess it is,' Alex replied, looking quickly away. So far this morning, she had kept things pretty well under control. 'I'll be in touch as soon as...' She stopped and clutched at the side of the boat as Bozo suddenly flung himself into the water and went swimming toward the shore as fast as he could go.

'Bozo, damn you, get back here!' Jake shouted, to no avail.

'What on earth made him do that?' Alex wondered aloud. Then she saw. 'No! Bozo, stop it!' She added her voice to Jake's at the sight of the dog lurching up the bank at top speed in pursuit of Murphy, who ran flat out and launched himself into the tamarack tree by the corner of the cottage porch. 'Get that dog out of here!' she screamed at Jake. 'He's put poor Murphy up a tree!'

'Hold the boat,' Jake said grimly, jumping out and throwing the line to Alex. 'I thought you said your cat was inside.'

'He must have jumped out of a window,' Alex replied. 'The old screens aren't very strong. He probably decided I was never coming back and he'd have to hunt for his living.' She watched as Jake, cursing vividly, sloshed his way to the shore, collared the big, wet dog and dragged him back toward the lake, then picked him up and deposited him in the boat.

'Why is it,' Jake said then, turning his scowl on Alex, 'that I seem to spend so much time in the lake with my clothes on since I met you?'

'Probably because you don't have the sense to wear a swimming suit when you go out in your boat?' Alex suggested.

'Neither do you,' Jake replied, looking down at her cut-off jeans, which were once again damp at the bottom edges. 'At least you didn't have to pick up a wet dog.' He looked at his own sodden shirt for a moment, then back at Alex, an evil grin suddenly lighting his face.

'Don't you dare!' Alex cried, reading his intentions. She started to swim away, but Jake caught her with one long lunge.

'Aha, now I've got you!' he cried triumphantly, laughing down at her as he held her suspended in waist-deep water. 'You haven't had one of my special flings in quite a while, have you?'

'And I don't want to! Ooooh!' Alex squealed as she flew through the air. She came up from her watery landing, spluttering in rage. 'You are absolutely retarded, Jake Jensen!' She paddled to his side and got to her feet again. 'How you can possibly manage to run a corporation escapes me completely!'

'Why do you think I need your help?' Jake asked with a teasing grin. He put his hands on her shoulders. 'I really think I should kiss you goodbye, don't you?'

'I certainly do not!' Alex cried. She started to back away, but found herself quickly grasped around the waist. 'No, Jake,' she said warningly, pushing her hands against his chest. 'You promised to treat me like any male employee. I'm sure you don't kiss them goodbye.' And, she thought, with a shiver of panic, not many of them would feel themselves responding to the almost tangible warmth emanating from that seductive smile of his.

'No,' Jake said with a sigh, 'but they don't look like you do. If they did, I probably would.' He put his fingers under Alex's chin and tipped her face toward his. 'Yes,' he said, 'I'm sure I would.' He began to lower his head towards her.

Alex felt her knees begin to tremble strangely. This, she decided, was going to have to stop. She had to think of something!

'Just a minute, Jake,' she said, pulling her head back as far as she could to evade his intentions. 'I'll let you kiss me if you promise that when you get back to New York you'll go in and give the head of the accounting department...' she searched her memory frantically for the name she had read ' . . . Ralph Grogan, isn't it? . . . a great big kiss.'

Jake stopped, his face so close that all Alex could see clearly were deep blue eyes fringed with thick black lashes, eyes that seemed to have magical lights playing in their translucent depths. 'All right,' he murmured, just before his lips met hers, 'I promise. But it's going to be a terrible shock to old Ralph.'

It was not a long kiss this time, but its warmth was so powerful that the chill of the lake water vanished from Alex's body in seconds and then reappeared like an Arctic blast when Jake released her, smiling that peculiarly trimphant smile of his.

'Have a safe trip home, Alex,' he said softly. 'I'll be talking to you soon.'

Alex stirred herself from contemplation of her response to Jake Jensen, and his obvious intention to dominate her sexually even if he could not to do so in other ways. It was beginning to look like karate lessons were in order. Jake simply would not take any other kind of no for an answer. But if he thought he could make light of her desires for equal treatment he was making a very big mistake.

'I plan to check with Mr Grogan,' she warned, lifting her chin and trying hard to glare at Jake as fiercely as he deserved. 'I'd better not find out you lied to me.'

'You won't,' Jake promised. He climbed into his boat and started the engine. 'See you later, Alex,' he called as, with a brief salute, he turned the boat and roared off across the lake.

Very strange, Alex thought, staring after him. She had a feeling that there was something about Jake Jensen that she did not understand at all, but maybe that was only because he was so mixed up that he wasn't comprehensible to anyone who was half-way normal. Still, his success with Jenstar was there for all to see. He must have a very different pesonality when he was at work. Maybe she'd be able to understand that side of him a little better.

'Yow-ow-ow!' A loud howl from the shore made Alex turn quickly around. There was Murphy, pacing along the edge of the water, looking desperately toward her.

'Murphy!' Alex cried, starting toward him hurriedly. 'You poor baby, are you all right? Guess what, love, it's going to be fish and chips for you from now on. Maybe even lobster once in a while! What do you think of that?'

Murphy eyed his dripping mistress critically as she came to shore, then silently turned and ran toward the cottage, his tail up like a flag.

I guess, Alex thought as she followed him, that a can of tuna in hand is worth several lobsters in the future.

CHAPTER FIVE

'WE'RE home, Murphy,' Alex announced shortly before noon the next day. She had been able to manage an early getaway from Tamarack, thanks to a stroke of luck in finding an advertisement in the *Tamarack Times* from a woman looking for cleaning work. A phone call arranged for a moving company to come and box up all of the family treasures, except the old ledger, and bring them to Minneapolis for storage. She and her mother could then go over the things together at some later date.

She turned the key in the lock and opened her door. Inside she stopped, frowning uneasily. She was sure she had left the shade curtains pulled down on the south side to keep out the sun. And what was that window in the dining-room doing open? Was that a faint smell of *Magie Noire* in the air? Oh, no...

'Mother? Are you here somewhere?' Alex called.

'Alex, dear, are you back from the lake already?' Darlene Faraday emerged from the kitchen, tanned and sleek, blonde and chic, looking, Alex thought with amused despair, more like her older sister than her mother. At least she did not look tired and drawn as she did when an affair had just gone sour.

'If this is Minneapolis, I must be,' Alex said, giving her mother a warm hug and kiss. 'And to what do I owe the pleasure of this surprise? Did that fascinating man you met turn out to be a dud, after all?'

Darlene smiled and flushed with girlish confusion. 'Oh, no, not at all. Actually, he's had to go to New York, and so I thought I'd come here while you were gone and be alone to think things over. I have a feeling...this might be serious.'

'Really?' This was a first, Alex thought. Not that her mother hadn't had hopes of something serious before, but this was the first time she had responded by wanting to do some thinking about it.

'Yes. But don't just stand there, holding your suitcase, dear. Why don't I tell you about it while you unpack?'

'Good idea,' Alex agreed. She took her suitcase into her room and flung it on her bed. 'Who is this mysterious stranger?' she asked as she unzipped the case. 'Where did you meet him?'

'He's not really a stranger,' Darlene said, perching on the bed and smiling confidentially. 'Actually I've known him for years. We just happened to run into each other at a party at some big Hollywood producer's house. Your brother wangled some invitations and insisted that I go along. I was standing by the pool, drinking champagne and feeling absolutely overwhelmed by all of the glitter and glamour, when suddenly there was Peter, looking far better than he ever used to. With that silver hair and a sun-tan he's really handsome. The amazing thing was that he recognised me too, and came right over and started talking, just as if I were a regular at parties like that.' She fluttered her eyelashes. 'I'm beginning to feel like one, now. We've been to several more, even one out on some fabulous boat...'

'Whoa!' Alex interrupted, pausing in her unpacking and frowning at her mother. This was beginning to sound like something from a fairy-tale. Who was this Peter? Some Hollywood sleaze who had latched on to sweet, gullible Darlene, thinking that she had money? 'Go back a few steps. Just when did you used to know this Peter person? What does he do?'

Darlene looked uncomfortable. 'Actually, it was a long time ago, and I didn't know him very well. He was more of an acquaintance...' She changed her focus from Alex's frowning face to her suitcase. 'Wherever did you get that dreadful brassière?' she asked, lifting it from the bag. 'It looks like prison issue.'

'Never mind about that! It's a jogging bra,' Alex snapped, snatching it from her. 'Who is this Peter? I'm beginning to think he's an ex-convict.'

'His name is really Hans Peter,' Darlene said, massaging her hands together nervously, 'but everyone in Hollywood calls him either Peter or Pete. Back at Tamarack they used to refer to him as HP. His last name is Jensen. You do remember the Jensens, don't you, dear?' She raised her eyebrows and gave Alex a tentative smile.

'Oh, dear God...' Alex clapped her hand over her mouth and stared at her mother. This was more bizarre than anything she could have imagined! Her mother? Jake's father?

'There, you see? I was afraid you'd be upset. The Faradays always hated the Jensens, and I knew you'd probably learned that you ought to hate them too. That's why I didn't tell you right away who he was.'

'No, no, no! I'm not upset about that,' Alex said quickly, although after what Jake had said about his father she was afraid she had plenty to be upset about. But how was she going to explain? Oh, well, there was nothing to do but make it short and to the point. 'I don't hate the Jensens. In fact, I'm about to take a job with Jenstar and go to New York myself. I met Jake up at Tamarack and he offered me the chance to head up their Economic Forecasting division. It's too good an oppor-

tunity to pass up.' She paused and shook her head at
her mother's knowing smile. 'No, Mother, it's nothing
like that. Jake asked what I did and when he found out
what had happened to me at Northern Grain he practically forced the job on me. He's tired of the women's
groups giving Jenstar bad marks.'

'Hmmph!' Darlene scoffed. 'I'll bet if you were ugly
he wouldn't have offered you the time of day. Peter says
Jake's a regular Don Juan with the ladies.'

Like father, like son, Alex thought grimly. 'That's
what everyone says,' she replied with a shrug. 'Is there
any coffee? I got up awfully early and I have a lot to
do.'

'Of course. You know I always keep a pot on.' Darlene
led the way into the kitchen. 'I must say, you really
worked fast with Jake. Didn't you just go up there last
Saturday? How did you manage to get the cottage
cleaned up so fast? Did Jake come calling or did you go
to find him? Peter says he has a place on that little island
now. What is it like?'

Alex dealt with her mother's spate of questions as
quickly and sketchily as she could. 'So you see,' she
concluded, glancing at her watch, 'I have to pick up my
last cheque at Northern Grain, say goodbye to my
friends, talk to my landlord about subletting, do some
shopping, and start packing. Jake wants me in New York
as soon as possible, and I'm supposed to call him tomorrow and let him know when I'll be there. I may be
leaving as soon as this Friday, but I'm sure you can stay
for the rest of this month if you want to. The rent's paid
until then.'

'Leaving that soon? Hmmm. I wonder...' Darlene's
brow was puckered, her eyes having that withdrawn look
that Alex knew meant she was brewing some plan.

'I'm afraid so,' Alex said warily. 'Wonder what?'

'Well...maybe I'll come along to New York with you. Peter wanted me to come and move into his apartment with him, but I didn't want him to think I was too eager, so I turned him down. But if I were with you I'd have a nice safe place to stay, I could see him, and we could share the rent. Of course, I might not be with you for too long...' She gave Alex a sly smile. 'Would you mind?'

Amazing, Alex thought, staring at her mother. She was actually playing hard to get. She must be serious! But could she cope with a difficult new job and her mother's love-life at the same time? It would be nice to have someone to share the rent with, though, and Alex would be right there to give comfort when the affair ended, as she was sure it would.

'No, I wouldn't mind at all,' she finally answered. 'In fact, I think it's a great idea. We'll talk about it later, OK? Jake said he'd have someone try to locate an apartment for me. I'll let him know tomorrow that I'll be having a room-mate.'

'Good. Oh, one other thing.' Darlene's face turned very serious. 'Don't mention anything about me and Peter to Jake. It's kind of a...secret. I'll take care of letting Peter know I'm in New York when I'm ready.'

Alex frowned. Now what was her mother up to? 'All right,' she said, 'but isn't Jake apt to tell him? Do you want me to tell him not to?'

Darlene shook her head. 'I doubt he'll mention it. Just don't say anything.'

'Whatever you say,' Alex said with a shrug. She didn't have time to figure this little game out. 'Now I've got to go. I can hardly wait to see Noel Smith's face when he hears the news.'

'Wonderful. Run along, dear. Oh ... do stop somewhere while you're out and get some nicer underthings.
You're going to be an important executive now, and you
wouldn't want to have an accident and be found in
those ... well, drab things you have. I always buy Princess
Lydia's myself. They're very nice.'

'Yes, mother,' Alex sighed resignedly. 'I'm going to
need some other clothes, too. I'll take care of it
tomorrow.'

For the next twenty-four hours Alex felt as if she had
been caught in a whirlwind that at times made her
wonder if taking the job with Jenstar and trying to cope
with Jake's demands for her early arrival were worth the
trouble. However, Noel Smith's reaction when she made
her announcement to him more than made up for it. In
seconds his expression of pompous superiority disappeared. He registered first disbelief, then amazement,
then sheer, hateful envy. Even his nasty, petty remarks
on how Alex must have got the job did not bother her.
It was only what she would have expected of him, and
she laughed in his face and told him so, then turned on
her heel and left, feeling quite vindicated.

On Wedneday afternoon Alex put in her promised call
to Jake, finding it rather amazing that she was put
through immediately with a deferential, 'Certainly, Miss
Faraday.' She was feeling even more amazed when she
finally hung up.

'Is something wrong, dear?' Darlene asked as her
daughter stared vacantly into space, her hand still on the
telephone. 'Is my coming along a problem?'

'No, not at all. Jake said he was delighted to hear it.
It's just so ... so overwhelming.' As was everything about
Jake Jensen! 'Jake's sending one of the corporate jets
for us Friday morning, and we've got the loan of an

apartment on Central Park, complete with maid and butler and a chauffeured limousine! It belongs to a Jenstar executive named Dunsmoor who's on assignment in Paris and is using Jake's apartment there, so he owes Jake a turnabout. The chauffeur will meet us at LaGuardia. I'm to call Jake as soon as we get in.'

Alex shook her head, trying to erase the feeling of disbelief that all of this was really happening or going to happen. But even more unsettling than the facts of her rapidly changing life was the undeniable thrill that had started her heart racing at the sound of Jake's deep, soft voice. How on earth was she going to adjust to that, on top of everything else? 'I'm not sure I can cope with all that,' she muttered, sinking into a chair, still staring into space.

'What, life in the fast lane?' Darlene asked innocently. 'Goodness, dear, you'll have to get over that. Peter says that's one of the problems with women in business. They're so used to being subservient, they can't cope with success.' Her eyes glittered suddenly. 'Or is it Jake Jensen that you aren't sure you can cope with?'

'Of course I can cope with Jake Jensen!' Alex snapped, feeling suddenly irritated with herself. It was just the excitement of going to New York and starting a new job that had her momentarily unhinged. That was all. 'And with the rest of it, too. Now, where's my list of things to do? I haven't any time to waste. Oh, yes. Shopping's next. Want to come along?'

'I certainly do. We've got to get you properly outfitted to meet all of those captains of industry. They'll expect you to look like a Paris model and be as ruthless as Genghis Khan. I can help you with the model part, but you'll have to do the rest yourself.'

Where her mother got the fanciful notion about Genghis Khan, Alex was not sure, but she did feel like something between a Parisian model and Cinderella on Friday as Jason, a perfectly type-cast chauffeur, thin and distinguished-looking in his uniform, ushered her and her mother into the limousine and then placed Murphy in his travelling-box on the seat beside her with a haughty, 'Your cat, Miss Faraday.'

'Thank you, Jason. The cat's name is Murphy,' Alex said.

She had to suppress a giggle when Jason replied courteously, 'An excellent name for a cat.' What, she wondered as she smoothed the skirt of her new beige silk and linen suit, would Jason think if she had replied 'and Jason is an excellent name for a chauffeur'?

'Isn't New York exciting?' Darlene said, beaming at Alex and then turning her head rapidly back to peer out of the window. 'I haven't been here in so many years. Oh, look, there's the Empire State Building.' She gestured out the window and then looked back at Alex. 'I'm so glad you got your hair trimmed. It makes you look so cool and collected, even if you are feeling all full of butterflies. What did Mr Jensen say when you called?'

'His secretary took the message. He was in a meeting,' Alex answered. She had told her mother that twice before, but Darlene Faraday was so a-twitter over flying in a luxurious private jet and then being greeted like royalty, that she was almost flying herself. Alex's feeling was not one of butterflies, but rather of being under tight rein, an electric excitement dwelling just below the surface that she knew she must control. It would never do for her to turn into a babbling neophyte at all of these new and wondrous experiences. The jangle of a telephone in her ear almost undid her, and she glanced around quickly to see where the noise came from. A limousine with a telephone too? This was almost too much.

She had just spotted it on the wall to her right when Jason volunteered, 'That is probably a call for you, Miss Faraday.'

'Thank you, Jason,' Alex replied, picking up the receiver and saying 'Hello?' with as much aplomb as she could muster.

'Alex! Where are you?'

Alex's heart did a little cartwheel at the sound of Jake's voice. She took a deep breath and swallowed. 'Hello, Jake. Just a minute, I'll ask Jason.' A moment later she reported, 'We're on the Queens Expressway, almost to the turn off for the Queensboro Bridge.'

'Good. I'm not running too far behind schedule, then. I'll see you in a few minutes.'

There was a click as Jake apparently hung up. Alex shrugged and replaced her receiver in its cradle.

'That was Jake and all he said was that he'd see me in a few minutes,' she reported to her mother, who was watching her intently.

'Lovely. I'm anxious to see him again, too.' Darlene sat back, smiling, and Alex eyed her suspiciously, but said nothing. No doubt her mother was entertaining herself by fabricating some kind of romantic involvement between Alex and Jake, but Alex was not about to entertain Jason by discussing that misconception now. Instead she looked out of her window, trying to pick out the few landmarks that she knew, and thinking how much she had to learn about New York. Getting around town was going to be part of her job. Jason's services were definitely going to come in handy.

'Here we are, miss,' Jason said, stopping in front of an imposing old building. He opened the door, and the doorman rushed to assist them with their baggage, to usher them through the security doors, and then whisk them upwards from the marble and gilt entry lobby to the polished mahogany-walled foyer, with its deep red oriental rug and crystal chandelier, from which they entered their borrowed apartment.

'Pinch me,' Darlene whispered in Alex's ear as the door swung open and the butler, Hawthorne, bowed and then introduced them to the maid and housekeeper.

Her mother's comment brought back memories of Jake's pinch, and Alex nearly burst into nervous giggles, but managed to convert it to an exceptionally wide smile of greeting for the staff.

'Mr Jensen is waiting for you in the grand salon, Miss Faraday,' Hawthorne then announced. 'Right this way.'

The maid took charge of Murphy and the housekeeper escorted Darlene toward her room. Alex followed Hawthorne through an arched doorway where plaster cherubs tooted their horns above French-blue damask draperies, and into a huge, high-ceilinged room that could have been a museum of period furniture. There were crystal chandeliers, velvet upholstery in shades of blue and rose, and objects of polished brass or sparkling crystal on gleaming tables everywhere, all so artfully done that in spite of the number of pieces it seemed airy and uncluttered. It was, Alex decided as she paused in the doorway, the most beautiful room she had ever seen. It was also not a place she could possibly imagine herself living in. And Murphy... He could do a million dollars worth of damage in five minutes! She would have to warn the servants to keep him out of here.

Quickly she turned to address Hawthorne, but he had gone. She turned back at the sound of a chuckle and Jake's voice saying warmly, 'Hello, Alex. You look absolutely lovely.'

'Jake, I can't live here!' she blurted as he came towards her, his hands outstretched. 'Murphy'll wreck the place.' She felt like biting her tongue when Jake threw his head back and laughed heartily. 'I simply meant,' she said stiffly, 'that this room is as elegant as a palace, and, while I think it's very beautiful, I don't think Murphy will appreciate it. He's a very bourgeois cat.'

'You needn't explain,' Jake said, taking her hands in his and squeezing them gently. 'This room affects me the same way. Can you imagine Bozo in here?'

'Heavens, no!' Alex replied, suddenly aware of the warmth seeping up her arms from Jake's hands, the velvety softness of the deep blue of his eyes, and the incredibly handsome contrast of his tanned face above the snowy shirt and deep red tie that he wore with a midnight-blue suit. 'Wh-what shall I do...about Murphy?' she stammered dizzily. 'I don't want him to damage your friend's things.'

'Leave him to the servants,' Jake said, smiling as he pulled on Alex's hands and drew her closer to him. He bent his head, his cheek brushing against hers. 'They won't mind,' he whispered into her ear. 'Compared to the Dunsmoors' brats he should be a picnic.'

'Oh! I beg your pardon.'

At the sound of her mother's voice Alex started and turned away from Jake, feeling as guilty as if they had been caught in an embrace, and quite sure that her romantic mother would think it had been.

'Hello, Mother,' she said, pulling her hands free. 'Jake, do you remember my mother, Darlene Faraday?'

'It's been a long time,' he replied. 'I didn't expect her still to look like your older sister.'

At that gallant remark, Alex could see her mother fall under Jake's spell as if a hypnotist had given her a cue. She flushed and fluttered her eyelashes, staring at Jake entranced while he made several inconsequential remarks, concluding with, 'I'm afraid I'm going to spirit your daughter away for the day. Can I persuade you to join us for dinner tonight?'

Darlene's eyes lighted briefly and then flicked quickly back and forth from Jake to Alex. 'Oh, no, thank you. I'm afraid I'm too tired to go out tonight,' she demurred, smiling but avoiding Jake's eyes with a look toward Alex. 'Perhaps some other time.'

'Then you must promise to come to the party at my place next weekend,' Jake said. 'There will be a lot of interesting people there.'

'Oh, yes! I'd love to,' Darlene agreed quickly.

'We'd better be going,' Jake said then, putting an arm around Alex's shoulders. 'We have reservations for luncheon at the Tavern on the Green.' After the elevator doors had closed on them, he said thoughtfully, 'I'm glad your mother came to New York with you. I'd like her to get reacquainted with my father.'

At that remark Alex almost choked, but she managed to say blandly, 'That would be nice,' while thinking how strange it was that Jake apparently didn't know they were already 'reacquainted'. The Jensens must not communicate as well as she and her mother did. Either that, or his father had some reason for keeping the affair quiet. Only time would give the answer. Meanwhile, she would like to know what Jake had planned for the rest of the day.

'What,' she enquired, as Jake shepherded her from the elevator, 'is this mysterious spiriting away for the rest of the day all about? Do you always give new executives so much personal attention?'

'Always,' Jake said positively, ignoring Alex's suspicious look. 'We're the first team at Jenstar, and it's important that we know and understand each other well. As far as today is concerned, first we're going to have lunch, then we'll go to my offices so that you can sign your contract. After that, I'll show you your offices and introduce you to some of the people you'll be working with. Then I thought we'd do some shopping. You'll need something special for the party next week. The Press may well be on hand, and I want you to knock them dead. If you look like a sweet, innocent girl from Minnesota they'll eat you alive. Also, I'll begin briefing you on how to deal tactfully with the idiosyncrasies of the various board members and their wives, and not so tactfully with the media people. I'll try to protect you when I'm around, but I may not always be there when they are.'

Another limousine had appeared like magic, gliding up before the apartment building just as Jake and Alex emerged from the door. Jake held open the door for Alex, but instead of getting in she stood stiffly on the pavement, glaring at him. Of all the insufferably bossy, arrogant, overbearing men she had ever met, Jake Jensen certainly took the prize! What kind of a naïve idiot did he think she was?

'Am I to understand,' she demanded, her voice frigid, 'that you don't feel that I am capable of dressing suitably, being tactful, or fielding questions from the Press? Because, if that's the case, I doubt if I'm bright enough to do even the simplest job, let alone the one you're hiring me to do.'

'Get in,' Jake said gruffly. 'This is neither the time nor the place to argue about it.'

Alex saw him flick a glance toward the doorman and then back at her. Aha! The doorman must be someone who liked to spread gossip. She lifted her chin and raised her voice slightly.

'All right,' she said, 'but I still refuse to wear pink tights and spangles, and I think I should get an extra twenty thousand for walking that tightrope without a safety net.'

With that she ducked quickly into the car and then stared studiously out of the window as Jake followed her and slammed the door behind him.

'What in hell was that about?' he growled softly, sliding over close to her. 'Am I crazy, or did I hear you mention pink tights, spangles, and a tightrope act?'

'Both,' Alex replied, turning her head and finding Jake's face only inches from her own, a strangely quizzical look quirking one eyebrow up and one corner of his mouth down. Her senses went on full alert as she felt the power of his intense gaze. He looked, she thought with a little shiver, as if he had been trying to take command of her and had suddenly stepped off another ledge like the one at Tamarack Lake. He did not seem to be enjoying the experience. Well, that was just too bad! 'I was only giving the doorman something interesting to pass on,' she said, trying to pull her head back a little and finding the red leather interior of the limousine in the way. 'Now, where were we? Oh, yes, you were trying to straighten me out on several points, weren't you? What were they again?'

'You know every word that I said perfectly well,' Jake replied, his eyes narrowed and his nostrils flared as he breathed hard, his chest rising and falling visibly.

His eyes were dark and dangerously bright, the way they stared into Alex's without blinking making her wish there were a lot more room for retreat in the huge limousine. Then slowly they drifted downwards, stopping at her lips, staying there, his own mouth opening slightly as he licked his lips very deliberately. She could feel her lips part as if in response and her tongue flick across her bottom lip, which felt dry and swollen. It took a conscious effort to tuck her tongue back inside her teeth and close her mouth again. She had to clench her hands to keep from reaching up and laying her hand along his smooth cheek or taking one finger and tracing the outline of his lips that curved in such clear, wide lines above and below. And all the while he stared...and stared. Alex could feel her heart pounding as the tension between them built unbearably. Then suddenly it broke. The limousine had stopped and Jake looked away, watching the driver jump out.

Without looking at Alex he said gruffly, 'I warned you about baiting me. You'll have to pay for it later.'

With that he got out and helped her to follow, smiling as urbanely as if nothing at all had happened. 'Did you know,' he said conversationally, tucking his hand beneath her elbow, 'that this part of Central Park used to be the sheepfold where they kept the sheep that grazed in the sheep meadow over there?' He gestured past the building toward an open grassy area.

'Sheep?' Alex asked vaguely. She remembered all too vividly what had happened the last time Jake had accused her of baiting him. But she hadn't been! She was only trying to keep him from being obnoxiously over-bearing. Didn't he understand that?

'Yes, sheep,' Jake answered as they followed a waiter to their table. 'You know, those white, woolly crea-tures.' He grinned as Alex gave him a disgusted look. 'Well, you didn't look as if you knew what they were.'

'I know sheep, and I also know a wolf in sheep's clothing when I see one,' she replied, with a meaningful glance that made Jake grin unrepentantly. 'Now, how about starting over? I can't believe you really think I need help buying a dress, or that your board members are that eccentric. Just what is going on in that devious mind of yours?'

Jake leaned his chin on his hand, staring at Alex so unblinkingly that she finally looked away, her nerves tightening uncomfortably.

'My mind isn't devious at all,' he said seriously. 'You asked me to treat you like any male employee, and I agreed to try, as long as you act like one. But a male wouldn't have asked why I was giving him so much per-sonal attention. He would have assumed he deserved it. And he certainly wouldn't have made any remarks about pink tights and spangles.'

Alex slanted a look back at Jake through narrowed eyes. 'And I suppose you'd have offered to take a male shopping?'

Jake sighed, as if his patience were wearing thin. 'Probably not. But I might well have given advice on what to wear when he met the media and directors, as well as some tips on how to deal effectively with them. You're entirely too suspicious of everything I say and do. I have hopes that once you know me better you won't be.'

'I hope so, too,' she said, with a wry little smile, although privately she doubted it. Looking into those deep blue eyes was like looking into a continually shifting kaleidoscope; fascinating but impossible to predict from one moment to the next. Would any amount of getting to know Jake Jensen change that feeling? 'One thing I'm sure of,' she added, 'is that it can't be managed in just one day. Knowing each other that well, I mean.'

'Oh, no.' Jake shook his head, smiling that special, warm smile of his as he raised his glass of wine. 'I expect it may take a very long time. Therefore, I propose a toast to our long and happy association.'

Alex raised her glass and touched it to Jake's. 'Why not?' she said with a faint smile, although at the moment she could think of several possible answers to her own question.

CHAPTER SIX

'EXCELLENT,' Jake said, the look of self-satisfaction on his face reminding Alex of Murphy's expression when he brought the results of a successful mousing expedition to her for her approval.

In the conference room which adjoined Jake's office, Alex had just signed her contract in the company of two of Jenstar's corporate lawyers. Now, back in his office, she eyed him warily as he sat casually on the corner of his mammoth desk and grinned at her.

'I have now killed at least two birds with one stone,' he said, in response to Alex's questioning lift of her brows. 'First of all, I have proved that Jenstar does put women in top positions. Secondly...' his eyes sparkled with a delight that Alex would have described as positively evil '...I have become your boss.'

Alex felt herself tense involuntarily. Exactly what did he mean by that? Nothing good, she was sure, judging by the gleam in his eyes.

'Don't push your luck,' she warned. 'You're only my boss in things related to Jenstar, not my private life.'

'Ah, but almost everything in your life will be related to Jenstar from now on,' Jake replied easily, sliding off the desk and coming to stand in front of Alex. 'Even to what you'll wear to the party next week.' He put his hands on Alex's shoulders. 'I had in mind something with some of those spangles.'

'Sequins?' Alex glanced up at Jake and then looked quickly down again, feeling a little shiver go through her

83

at the deeply intense look he was giving her. He was still trying to get the upper hand...in everything! 'No, thanks,' she said tightly. 'I have something to wear. If you want to know me better, you should know that I'm not the sort of person to invest a month's salary in some outlandish dress to wear one time.'

'This one's on the company,' he said. 'Promotional expense.'

'No!' Alex stamped her foot and scowled up at him. 'You wouldn't do that for a male employee, and you are not going to do it for me, either! Now, if you don't mind, you were going to show me my offices.' She jerked her chin away as Jake tried to trap it with his fingers. 'Don't do that!'

'Then stop being unreasonable. We'd buy a membership in a suburban golf club for a male to lure him here, something I doubt you'd be interested in, but which would cost far more. So calm down and let's go. I'll show you your offices on the way out. They're on the floor below.'

'No dress!' Alex dug in her heels, refusing to move as Jake tugged at her arm. 'I have a perfectly beautiful and suitable dress that I just bought.'

'Is it sexy?'

Alex felt her cheeks grow heated as Jake changed his tactics, taking her face between both of his hands, his eyes wandering down to her lips.

'Yes, as a matter of fact, it is,' she replied, trying to ignore the various electrical charges that seemed to be firing off in different parts of her body. 'It's sort of Grecian and clingy and shimmery blue.'

'That description creates some interesting images.'

Alex tried to back away, but found that she could not unless her neck stretched. She put her hands on Jake's wrists and tried to move them. It was useless, and all of the time the heat from his hands seemed to be spilling over into more and more of her body. She could feel beads of perspiration form on her upper lip as his eyes zeroed in on her lips.

'Your behaviour is not appropriate for a boss, *sir*,' she said hoarsely, putting her hands between them. 'I can get out of my contract if you keep this up.'

'No, you can't,' Jake replied with a crooked smile. 'I'll make it company policy, and kiss every new employee, male and female, in all of Jenstar if I have to. Besides, you owe me one from earlier and...' he put one hand behind Alex's head now and lowered his lips close to hers '...we owe it to each other to relieve some of the tension.'

Relieve tension! Alex felt as if she were a spring being wound, and Jake was the key. She tried to twist her head away, but found it turned inexorably back by Jake's hand. 'Don't!' she got out, but her voice was a tiny whisper, her field of view completely filled by black-fringed pools of deep, translucent blue and a mouth that looked as soft and warm as a sun-ripened plum.

'Don't fight it, Alex,' Jake said softly, his lips brushing hers. 'I don't intend to lose this battle.'

With that his lips possessed hers firmly, and his arms tightened their hold with almost crushing strength. I can't let him keep doing this to me, Alex thought, trying to ignore the echo in her ears of her pounding heart and the other sensations that told her that her body had quietly disconnected itself from her mind. Then, just as quietly it seemed, it took over. Taste him, hold him, be close, it said seductively. Feel how big and strong and warm he is. Put your arms around him. There, that's better. You've wanted to touch his hair and see if it felt as satiny smooth as it looks. Go ahead.

As if in a dream, Alex obeyed, all of her senses responding so acutely they seemed magnified. There was a clean, spicy smell mingled with the sweet warmth of Jake's kiss. There was the hard, firm pressure of his body against her. He wants me, she thought dizzily. She could tell, almost as clearly as if there were no barrier of clothing between them. And she wanted him, more than she had thought it possible to want a man. When his hand slid inside her blouse, she drew in her breath sharply. She felt as if she would explode with wanting him. It would be so lovely if there were nothing between them, if she could feel every inch of his warm, strong body...

Oh, lord, what am I thinking of? she wondered as Jake pulled his head back and smiled at her, his eyes drowsily warm.

'Whoa,' he said huskily, as if he had read her thoughts. 'We don't have time now, but we will soon, I promise.'

'D-don't be so presumptuous,' Alex stammered, her cheeks flaming.

'Oh, Alex,' Jake said, pulling her against him again and burying his cheek against her hair, 'what are you so afraid of? Me, or yourself? We're two adults who want each other desperately. We already know that about each other. Why does that frighten you so much?'

Alex stood very still, her head against Jake's chest, listening to the strong, fast beating of his heart. How did he make her feel this way? How did he create in her desires so strong they took her breath away? It seemed that all he had to do was to touch her and she was in a spin. Well, if sex was all that Jake Jensen wanted, he needn't have hired her for this job, and it was the job that she was here for. He had no right to do this to her, no right at all! It wasn't fair. And it was frightening. Tears sprang to Alex's eyes unbidden and she gulped back a sob.

'What's wrong?' Jake asked, peering instantly into her face.

'You are!' Alex cried, pushing him away. 'It's no wonder I'm suspicious of your motives! You keep pushing and pushing. Maybe there is some kind of physical attraction between us, but that's not what I'm here for, and... I have so much to learn, so much to do. Just leave me alone for a while. Let me get used to things, get started on my job. You did hire me to do a job, didn't you? It wasn't just an excuse to get me here so you could keep trying to seduce me, was it? Because, if it was, I'm getting out of here right now, contract or no contract, and I'll tell the whole world that everything they've said about you is true... that you really think there's only one thing women are good for! I was beginning to think it wasn't true, that you were willing to treat me like an intelligent human being instead of just a sex object, but now I'm not so sure.'

'Good God, Alex, of course it's a real job, one of the most important at Jenstar!' Jake's expression was so sincerely contrite that Alex found it difficult not to believe him, especially when he rubbed one hand across his eyes and shook his head. 'I'm sorry, Alex, I really am. It's just that...' He shook his head again and sighed, leaving the sentence unfinished. 'Forgive me?' he asked, smiling that crooked little smile again.

'I guess so,' she replied, dabbing at her tears with the handkerchief he offered her, at the same time wondering if Jake were really as remorseful as he looked. Most likely he was eager to get back in her good graces so he could misbehave all over again.

'Good.' The clouds left Jake's countenance as if by magic. 'At least you admit to some kind of attraction to me,' he said with a grin that was not little-boyish at all. 'That's a lot better than the unimproved idiot you called me not long ago.'

'Maybe I'm just perverse. Anyway, I'd be stupid to deny the obvious, wouldn't I?' Alex said tightly. 'However, whether I do or not is beside the point. I am not about to let it interfere with my ability to do the job I came here for, and I suggest you try to remember what I'm here for, too. I can't work either for you or with you if you're going to pounce on me every time I come into your office.'

'Yes, ma'am,' Jake said soberly. 'We'll make those the magic words. If I make a wrong move just say "don't pounce" and I'll stop dead in my tracks.'

His eyes twinkled as Alex eyed him doubtfully and said, 'I think it might be more to the point if I take a karate course so I can fend you off.'

Jake's smile widened. 'I could teach you what I know. I've got a brown belt myself.'

'You would,' Alex retorted. 'I'll just have to get a black belt.' She took a mirror from her bag and inspected the damage to her make-up, which was minimal. 'All right,' she said. 'Let's go.' She gave Jake a sideways glance. 'You have given up on that dress project?'

'I thought my capitulation was obvious,' Jake replied with a chuckle. 'However,' he said as they went out the door and past his austere-looking, grey-haired secretary, 'I did think you'd look fantastic in a flesh-coloured body-stocking with a few strategically placed patches of red spangles.'

Alex could see his secretary's reflection in one of the many mirrors in some columns near Jake's private elevator. Her mouth was hanging wide open.

'I think you almost shocked your secretary out of her socks,' Alex scolded as the elevator doors slid shut. 'It will probably take me years now to convince her that I'm not a scarlet woman.'

'Maybe it would be easier to become one,' Jake teased, chuckling as Alex shot him a dark look.

'If I were interested in taking the easy way I wouldn't be here now,' she said with a meaningful lift of her brows.

The truth of that statement was borne out to Alex as, with Jake at her elbow, she toured the marvellous facilities that were to be hers. She was moving into a job many times bigger than the one she had left. The staff she was inheriting were young and friendly, but obviously curious about who she was and how she happened to be replacing their former chief. Sensing this, Jake called a small group of them into Alex's office and gave them a brief but flattering description of her capabilities.

'Miss Faraday already knows that getting the report on Peach Records shaped up has first priority,' he said. 'Have you people any progress to report?'

There was a general negative murmuring, until one bright-looking young man spoke up.

'We still haven't cracked Mr Jackson's code,' he said, 'but I've already started gathering some new data.'

'Code?' Alex questioned.

'Why don't you explain it to Miss Faraday?' Jake suggested. 'It will give her something to think about over the weekend. Alex, I'll go back to my office and you can join me when you're through here.' He grinned as

Alex shot him a dark look. He certainly wasn't giving her any time to settle in!

For almost an hour, Alex discussed the problems of the Peach Records report, discovering that her predecessor had apparently concealed a great deal of relevant data on the company by coding his files with some bizarre system no one could decipher.

'He never let any of us see them,' complained an attractive little brunette. 'He did all of the data gathering himself, since it was so important to Mr Jensen.'

'If what he found is anything like what I have, we've got a real mess on our hands,' said the bright-looking young man. 'Lorna Beauregard isn't much of a businesswoman.'

Lorna Beauregard? Alex's ears perked up at the sound of that name. She was the woman in the magazine picture. Jake Jensen's latest 'hot item', according to Sarah. So Lorna was the owner of Peach Records, and it didn't look like a winner, even though her predecessor had tried to make it appear to be. How fascinating! This turn of events would bear some close scrutiny. Jake had never mentioned Lorna at all. Just what might he have up his sleeve?

'Why don't you give me a printout of what you have?' she suggested smoothly. 'I'd like to look it over, so I'll be ready to go on Monday. And let me have a copy of those codes, too. Maybe I'll have a lucky inspiration.' She took the copies and tucked them into her bag. 'I'll see you all Monday morning,' Alex said to the group, who were watching her alertly, 'and we'll get right down to business.'

After everyone had left, Alex sat and stared into space. Why hadn't Jake mentioned that Lorna Beauregard owned Peach Records? Was he trying to hide something? No, she decided, probably not. If she was a country music fan, she'd probably have known it, and Jake didn't know she wasn't. However, if the Peach Records report she had seen was not only poorly done, but entirely wrong, that might mean something more sinister. If Jake knew, or suspected as much, why hadn't he told her? She shook her head. Men! He was probably so wrapped up in his lady love that he didn't know. Even the best businessmen could go blind and dumb when passions entered in. Well, if it turned out that Lorna Beauregard's company was a poor investment, he'd just have to bite the bullet. Alex Faraday wasn't going to compromise her integrity just to keep Jake Jensen's love-life running smoothly! She stood up, chewing her lip, then took a deep breath and stretched to relax her tense muscles. It wouldn't do for Jake to suspect what she'd heard. After all, she wasn't sure of anything yet. She found her way to the executive elevator, and was soon back at Jake's office.

'Mr Jensen has someone with him,' his secretary told Alex, her mouth in a tight, disapproving line. 'I'll let him know you're here.'

A moment later Jake's door opened, and he came out, his arm around none other than Lorna Beauregard, whose doll-like form and mop of copper hair were even more striking in person than in a photograph. For a moment Alex was stunned, but she took advantage of Jake's momentary self-conscious straightening of his tie to gather her wits and smile brightly, as if she were delighted to see the famous singer, and not even slightly surprised to find her at Jake's office. In reality she was having a hard time recovering from an initial impression that this sulky-faced little woman was a strange companion for the warm and virile Jake.

'Alex,' Jake said finally, clearing his throat, 'I'd like you to meet Lorna Beauregard. She's...er...an old friend of mine. If you're a country fan, you've surely seen her on television. Lorna, this is Alexis Faraday, Mr Jackson's replacement.'

Alex managed to beam at the woman, who was clutching Jake's arm as if it were a life preserver. 'Of course,' she said, extending her hand to see if Lorna could let go of Jake long enough to be polite. 'This is a real honour, Miss Beauregard.'

Lorna eyed her coldly, but forced her mouth into a smile. 'Ah'm delighted,' she drawled, shaking Alex's hand very limply, Alex thought, for someone who had had such a death grip on Jake. 'Ah do hope you all'l be able to do a better job on the Peach Records report.'

'Lorna owns Peach Records,' Jake interceded quickly, watching Alex closely, as if waiting for a reaction.

How interesting, Alex thought. Jake didn't think she knew. And judging from his expression, he didn't think she'd heard about his romantic entanglement with Lorna, either. Maybe if he thought she'd known both, she'd soon find out why he hadn't told her. Perhaps it had something to do with that option he'd mentioned.

'Of course,' Alex said, giving Jake a reproving look. She beamed at Lorna again. 'I plan to begin working on the report immediately.'

'It has to be ready for the board meeting, doesn't it, sugah?' Lorna said, batting her eyelashes toward him.

Sugah? How saccharinely sickening! Alex thought. But before Jake could reply she said quickly, 'No problem, Miss Beauregard. I'm known for my speed and efficiency.' She had to dig her fingernails into her palms to keep from laughing at the look of bafflement on Jake's face. He looked like a movie director, whose scene had completely got away from him. Did he have some ridiculous idea that she was so smitten with him that working on a report for his lady love's company would bother her?

She was still wondering about that when he returned from escorting Lorna to the elevator. He looked at her curiously as he took her arm to lead her into his office.

'I didn't realise you were aware of Lorna's association with Peach Records,' he said, as soon as the door closed behind them.

'My goodness, yes!' Alex exclaimed. 'And you and Miss Beauregard were the talk of all the ladies back at Northern Grain. She's so much prettier in person, though.'

Jake frowned, his eyes flicking over Alex's face suspiciously. 'I hope you don't believe everything you read in those gossip columns.'

'Shouldn't I?' She leaned forward and peered at Jake's cheek. 'You'd better wipe off that lipstick. I don't think tangerine is your shade.'

'No, you shouldn't!' Jake said firmly, whipping out a handkerchief and rubbing his cheek firmly. 'I wouldn't want you to get the impression that I have a vested interest in how that report comes out.'

'You don't? You said something about an option,' Alex replied.

'Of course not. The option is only relevant to the timing,' Jake said, fixing Alex with an intense stare. 'However, I want you to be especially careful not to leak anything about the results of your findings to anyone before the board meeting. Is that clear?'

Alex frowned. Jake would persist in telling her things she didn't need to be told. 'I wouldn't think of it. That wouldn't be ethical,' she snapped. 'But I'll give my staff an extra warning if you think it's necessary.'

'It may be. There will be people who try to find out,' Jake said seriously, 'and a lot of damage could result if they do. I've got until the board meeting to try to prevent it permanently.' At Alex's questioning look he smiled suddenly. 'I can't explain further. Just do your job and I'll do mine, and we'll hope for the best.'

'That suits me perfectly,' Alex agreed with a shrug. After all, that was what she was here for. It did sound as if Jake suspected she might produce a very different report and was bracing himself for trouble with Lorna. For his sake, she hoped it wouldn't be, but for her own... Good heavens, what was she thinking of now? Just because seeing the two of them together had made her stomach churn didn't mean she had designs on Jake Jensen! Lorna Beauregard just didn't look like his type, that was all. She'd never have believed he'd fall for someone who flapped their eyelashes and called him 'sugah'!

'Good girl,' Jake said, giving Alex's shoulders a squeeze. 'Now, how about some dinner? I think we've had enough shop talk for today, don't you?'

Alex slanted a look up at him, suddenly unable to resist tweaking him about Lorna's pet name for him. 'Definitely,' she said, fluttering her eyelashes furiously and clutching at his arm. 'Where are we going, sugah?' The mischievous sparkle which had been missing from Jake's eyes since Alex had returned from her meeting reappeared.

'So you *are* jealous,' he said, grinning down at her.

'Jealous? Don't be ridiculous,' Alex said with a disdainful arch of her brows. How like Jake to think that! 'I was only trying out an obviously successful technique, in case I might want to use it some time. On someone else. Where are we going for dinner?'

'To my apartment, pussy cat,' Jake replied, turning on his sexiest voice and smile. 'I want to keep you all to myself. Besides, I thought you might never have been to a real New York penthouse, and you'd enjoy it. It's only three buildings up from where you're living, you know.'

'Oh, is it?' Alex replied vaguely, feeling the situation suddenly slipping from her grasp. 'I'm sure it will be...very interesting.' She wrenched her gaze away from those entrancing blue eyes as her cheeks began to feel warm, annoyed with herself and annoyed with Jake, too. She ought to scold him for looking at her like that, when he was practically engaged to another woman. She ought to tell him she'd feel a lot safer at some nice, busy restaurant. She did neither. She would, she resolved, learn to deal with this ridiculous physical response to Jake. If she couldn't, working for him was going to be quite a strain. Especially if he married Lorna Beauregard. That problem, however, was in the future. Right now, she had to survive a romantic dinner alone with him at his penthouse. Already she was feeling strange vibrations from just the touch of his big, warm hand enclosing hers as they walked to the elevator. This could be a very long evening.

CHAPTER SEVEN

IT was, in fact, one of the shortest-seeming evenings on record, Alex mused as she greeted Hawthorne after Jake's pleasant but formal goodnight. Could it really be almost midnight?

'Is my mother still up?' she asked.

'Mrs Faraday went out for the evening with Mr Peter Jensen,' Hawthorne replied. 'She hasn't returned yet.'

'Oh, really? That's . . . nice.' So much for playing hard to get, Alex thought. Darlene must have called Peter, after all. 'I don't think I'll wait up. Come along, Murphy. Goodnight, Hawthorne.'

'Goodnight, Miss Faraday.'

Alex walked slowly down the long, panelled hallway to the satin and lace lushness of her borrowed bedroom, feeling exhausted physically, but with her mind still working full tilt. She flopped down on her bed and began absently stroking Murphy's soft coat as he purred his happiness at her return.

'You know, Murphy,' she said softly. 'I don't understand that man at all.'

The evening at Jake's penthouse had not gone at all as Alex had expected. He had not made a single pass at her. They had compared notes on tastes in food over the excellent dinner that Jake's cook had prepared. After dinner, Jake had put on records of the piano music of Beethoven and they had discussed classical music and the other arts. There had been no mention at all of country music. To the accompaniment of Bach's

Brandenburg Concertos they had wandered into the topics of history and philosophy. While looking at the lights of New York from Jake's terrace garden their talk had changed to their own histories in the years since they had clashed on the raft at Tamarack Lake. It was strange how much in common they had had, each with a parent suffering from the loss of their spouse to worry over, both workaholics who often longed to get away to some quiet place.

'What am I doing here?' Alex had said whimsically, after describing the kind of place she would like to have in the country. 'I think I'll tear up my contract and go somewhere and raise chickens.' It was then that Jake had invited Alex to accompany him on the morrow to a farm in Connecticut that he was thinking of buying.

'I'd like your reaction to it,' he said. 'I'm afraid I may be so anxious to find a place in the country that's fairly close to New York City that I'm overlooking some major flaws.'

Somehow, Alex doubted that he was, but she agreed to go none the less. She had begun to see facets to Jake Jensen that she hadn't suspected during the brief sojourn at his cottage. In fact, her evening at his penthouse had been one of the most pleasant she had ever spent with a man. The tension generated from keeping her guard up in expectation of some sexual interplay had begun to ebb somewhere between Beethoven and Bach, and by the end of the evening she was feeling almost completely relaxed. Total relaxation with Jake would be next to impossible. His presence was too electric, and there was her strong reaction to the way he looked and sounded that continued of its own accord, no matter how serious the conversation. Her pulse would quicken when he smiled in that certain way he had, one side

quirking up more than the other, and a funny little
tingling would squiggle from her head to her toes when
his laugh rang out, deep and strong.

'I'll have to get over that, won't I?' she said to Murphy,
pushing herself from the bed and beginning to undress.
Jake was spoken for, and apparently, now that he knew
that she knew it, he wasn't going to try his tricks any
more. He hadn't even kissed her goodnight. The same
man who earlier in the day had promised he'd take her
to bed quite soon! If that wasn't a quick change!

'Don't look so disappointed,' Alex said, with a wry
grimace at her reflection in the mirror as she brushed
her hair. 'You're the one who wanted to be treated like
an intelligent human being and not a sex object, aren't
you?' She did not answer her own question, afraid that
an honest answer might reveal something she did not
want to think about just now. Instead, she thought, she
might well wonder how her mother was faring with Peter
Jensen. It was past midnight, and she still hadn't returned. If Darlene married Peter, that would make her
Jake's stepsister. Could she ever feel like a sister to Jake?
Oh, darn, there she was, back on that track again!

After a night of restless sleep, Alex was still feeling a
bit groggy when, in her robe, she wandered into the
dining-room for breakfast. Eight o'clock had come far
too soon, but Jake had promised to pick her up at nine
o'clock sharp. A strong cup of coffee was definitely in
order. To her amazement, her mother was already at the
table, looking bright and wide awake.

'I didn't expect to see you up this early,' Alex said,
sinking into a chair and helping herself to a slice of toast.

'Peter's taking me out sightseeing today,' Darlene replied, beaming happily. 'We had such a lovely time last
night. Dinner and dancing at the Waldorf.'

'Sounds lovely. When did you call Peter?'

'Oh, I didn't call him. Someone told him I was here and he called as soon as he found out.'

'Jake must have called him. He said something about getting you and his father together.' Alex frowned. 'He probably called when I was meeting with my staff.'

Darlene shrugged. 'Could be, but I doubt it. Peter told me a while back that they're hardly speaking to each other. He didn't say what the problem was, though.'

'Maybe it's been straightened out,' Alex said. She finished off a cup of coffee and stood up. 'I'd better get dressed. Jake's taking me to see a farm in Connecticut he's thinking of buying. I don't know when we'll be back.'

'Have a good time, dear,' Darlene said with a smile. 'I'll be leaving in a few minutes. We're going to take an early ride around the harbour and look at the Statue of Liberty.'

'You have fun, too,' Alex said, dropping a kiss on her mother's forehead. It was such a pleasure to see Darlene looking so happy after her years of pain and disappointment. How she hoped that things would continue to go smoothly for her and Peter.

'Did you know that your father has my mother in tow on a tour of the city today?' Alex asked Jake as they headed north out of New York City toward Connecticut. There was no chauffeured limousine today. Jake was driving his own Porsche.

'Really? That's great,' Jake replied. 'Dad knows every nook and cranny of the city. He loves it.'

'What does he think of your buying a farm?' Alex asked.

'He doesn't know,' Jake replied, with a sideways glance at Alex. 'We haven't been communicating much recently. I had my secretary let him know your mother was in town.'

Alex looked at Jake thoughtfully as he watched the road ahead. There was a grim set to his jaw, and a frown had settled between his brows. What on earth could be wrong between him and his father? She was trying to think of some tactful way to ask when Jake suddenly continued on his own.

'I think your mother's coming to New York may turn out to be almost as good a stroke of luck as my finding you at Tamarack. Dad's been needing the company of someone more his own age.'

The implications of that statement were obvious, Alex thought, in light of the comment he had made at Tamarack about his father's lust for pretty girls. She said, 'That must mean you didn't approve of some of his previous choices.'

Jake made an impolite, snorting sound and flicked another quick glance in Alex's direction as they sped along. 'That's putting it mildly. I suppose you might as well hear it from me, before the gossip-mongers get to you. Until a few months ago, when I stepped in, he was planning to marry Lorna Beauregard.'

'Oh, my!' Alex said, shocked at the revelation. Jake had actually stolen Lorna from his father! No wonder the two weren't speaking! 'That is sticky, isn't it?' And it might be a problem for her mother, too. 'Is he still carrying a torch, do you think?'

'I wish I knew,' Jake said glumly. 'So far he hasn't been willing to discuss it rationally. Maybe your mother will help him to see the light.'

'Maybe,' Alex said with a sigh. It sounded very much as if Darlene was walking right into a veritable soap opera triangle. She looked over at Jake, who took his eyes off the road for a moment and gave her a warm smile.

'Let's let our parents take care of their own problems for the rest of the day,' he suggested. 'I'll tell you about the farm, instead. It's been a real, working dairy farm until this past year, so it's not one of those duded-up retreats. There's a nice big house, a huge barn with a silo, and several other small buildings. It's tucked away in a little valley with a stream running through it. Even though it's not far from the more settled areas, it seems very private.'

'From what you say, I can't imagine finding any fault with it,' said Alex. 'It sounds lovely. How did you discover it?'

'It discovered me,' Jake said with a grin. 'It belongs to the parents of one of the engineers at Jenstar Electronics, and he told me about it. His parents wanted to retire and start travelling, but they refused to sell to someone who wanted to turn the farm into a condo development, and no one wants to go into dairy farming right now. When he told me about it, I put down some option money before I even saw it.'

They arrived at the farm before noon, and it was even lovelier than Alex had imagined. The house sat square and comfortable-looking beneath huge old maple trees, a wide porch overlooking the rocky slope down to a small pond, where the creek had been dammed.

'It needs redecorating,' Jake said, as he opened the door. 'I'd like to keep it pretty much the way it is, except for fresh paint and wallpaper.'

'Maybe you should ask Lorna what she'd like,' Alex suggested.

Jake shrugged. 'Maybe,' he said. 'But since she isn't here, why don't you tell me what you think?'

'That's rather beside the point, isn't it?' Alex said tightly. She could already tell that it was the kind of place she'd always dreamed of. It was a family sort of house, roomy but not too fancy, and the setting was perfect. Spending very much time thinking about the place in terms of herself and the handsome man at her side might be dangerous.

'I'll check the kitchen out,' she said, moving ahead of Jake. 'Kitchens are always important.' She hurried down the central hallway and found the large, country kitchen, complete with a huge stone fireplace. 'Perfect,' she said, poking her head through a doorway at the side. 'Oh, isn't this nice? A pantry. Plenty of cupboards.' She looked at Jake, who was watching her from near the fireplace, a bemused smile on his face. 'Great kitchen,' she said, quickly looking away before her nerves could start that ridiculous quivering they did when he looked at her like that.

They toured the rest of the high-ceilinged old house, which had four large bedrooms and two rather plain bathrooms upstairs, and a spacious living-room, dining-room and den downstairs, in addition to the kitchen. It was, Alex noted, much less elegant than Jake's other abodes. While she found it pleasant and comfortable, she couldn't imagine Lorna Beauregard in it.

'Well,' Jake said, as they stood again at the bottom of the stairs, 'what do you think now? Is there anything that needs a major change?'

'Nothing I'd change, except that disgusting, green, splotchy wallpaper in the front bedroom,' Alex replied. 'It looks like a fungus. But I still think you should have

Lorna look it over. Women like to have a say in such things, you know.'

Jake grinned and shook his head. 'She'll just have to take it the way I want it,' he said. 'Come on. Let's have a look at the barn.'

Alex gave him a disgusted look, but followed along. Poor Lorna! Jake was certainly planning on being the lord and master in that household. But then, maybe someone who called him 'sugah' wouldn't mind...

Inside the immense barn, with its long row of stanchions for cattle, it was as dark and silent as a cathedral. Alex felt uneasy, and looked up to find Jake staring at her.

'What's wrong?' he asked. 'You look sad.'

'I don't know,' she said, frowning. 'Something doesn't feel right. It's too quiet and deserted. It needs some cows.'

'Cows,' Jake repeated thoughtfully. 'Yes, I think you're right. If I can get someone competent to live in the small house at the back of the property and take care of them I'll get some.'

He grinned as Alex clapped her hands enthusiastically and exclaimed, 'Oh, good!'

'Aren't you worried about whether Lorna will approve?' he asked.

'Why should I be if you're not?' she retorted. 'You'll have to promise to let me visit if you get some.'

'That's a promise,' Jake said soberly. 'Want to climb up to the hay loft?'

'Sure. That's why I wore jeans,' Alex replied. 'You're always supposed to climb into the hay mow when you visit a farm.' She started up the ladder, with Jake close behind her. 'Phew, it's warmer up here,' she said as she gained the top and surveyed the long loft beneath the vaulted roof of the barn. 'You still have some hay for your cows.' She pointed to the pile of bales at one end of the loft.

'I wonder if it's good,' Jake said. He walked over to the pile and picked up a bale. 'Seems to be all right.' Then he climbed up on the pile and made his way to the very end of the loft, where a small, hexagonal window showed a patch of bright blue sky. 'Come on up here,' he called, looking back at Alex. 'The view is spectacular. Be careful,' he added, as a bale tipped beneath Alex's feet and she almost fell.

'Oh, look at that!' Alex exclaimed, as she finally gained her footing and stood beside Jake on the very top bale. Over the treetops they could see the little stream meandering down the narrow green valley, and in the distance the white church steeple of a tiny New England town. 'What a picture,' she said, looking up at Jake and smiling. 'Can you imagine how it must look in the winter?'

'Perfectly lovely,' Jake replied, his eyes not leaving Alex's face.

Alex felt a shiver go through her at that familiar, intense look that lingered now on her lips. He wouldn't... would he? He had been so well behaved lately. But his eyes were getting darker, and she could feel her own pulse quickening. She had better move away while there was still time.

She took a tiny step backwards, Jake's arm came out to stay her, and suddenly the bale they were standing on tipped crazily and they fell. Head over heels they went, together, down the pile of hay, Jake clutching her close to protect her. They came to a stop on a pile of loose hay from some broken bales at the bottom.

'Alex, are you all right?' Jake asked. He gently brushed some hay from her face and peered anxiously into her eyes.

'I think so,' Alex replied, blinking to clear the hay dust away. She was still held fast in Jake's arms, his face only inches from hers. His black hair was laced with stems and leaves from the hay, and on his cheek was a long scratch. 'Are you?' she asked. 'I think you took most of the bumps.' She reached up and gingerly felt his cheek. 'Does that scratch hurt?'

'Not a bit,' he replied, smiling and catching her hand in his. He lifted her fingers to his lips and nibbled on them teasingly, at the same time tightening his grip with his other arm behind her.

'Now, Jake...' Alex began, as suddenly her body forgot the feeling of falling and concentrated on the body beside it, and her mind registered the fact that the fall hadn't changed his intentions at all.

'Shhh,' Jake said, putting his finger to her lips. 'Can't you see that fate wanted us to be here like this?'

'Fate, nothing. It was the law of gravity,' Alex protested, trying to tear her eyes from Jake's as he stroked her cheek with the back of his fingers. She made a vain attempt to wriggle free, but found that her body did not have much wriggle left in it.

'That's better,' Jake said, as she lay still and stared at him, her lips feeling swollen and her body increasingly warm.

Why doesn't he just kiss me and get it over with? she wondered, her tongue flicking nervously across her lips.

'Alex,' Jake said softly, tugging her knitted shirt loose at the back and sliding his hand up beneath it to unfasten her bra, 'I want to kiss you all over, I want to make love to you, but I won't go any further than you want me to. All right?'

Alex had no time to protest before his lips closed over hers, sending a current of excitement zinging through her that met the one generated by his exploring hand and closed a circuit of ecstatic impulses. She felt assaulted on all sides by tantalising sensations. Even as her tongue tried to catch and taste the inner secrets of Jake's deliciously warm mouth she pressed against the hand enclosing her breast. When her shirt was raised upwards and soft lips followed that hand, she closed her eyes and laid her head back, watching the strange celestial fireworks that accompanied the exploding waves of sensation those lips produced. Currents of longing shot downward as Jake's hand slipped inside her jeans. She didn't want him to stop. She didn't ever want him to stop. A little moan escaped her lips as her zipper slid down and she arched toward Jake's exploring hand. Soon there would be no turning back. Soon she would be his...

Dear lord, what was she thinking of?

'No, Jake, no!' she cried, thrusting him from her and pulling herself to a sitting position. 'I can't! I just can't.' He was another woman's man, and even if he didn't care, she did. 'I'm sorry,' she said, feeling utterly miserable at the cold, frustrated look on Jake's face. 'I should have stopped you sooner. I just don't go for casual sex. I never have.'

'Then you should learn not to react as if that's exactly what you do want every time I get near you,' he snapped.

'Maybe I could if you didn't always grab me and start pawing me,' she snarled back, jumping to her feet and beginning to straighten her clothes. 'I pity poor Lorna, trying to keep tabs on you.'

'Leave Lorna out of this!' Jake glared at her, then got up and began brushing hay from his clothes. 'Explain to me why you're now wearing lacy underwear if you didn't intend me to see it.'

'Because my mother told me to,' Alex replied. 'Not that it's any of your business.'

'A likely story,' Jake scoffed. 'You were damned well hoping I'd see it! Just like you're hoping that one of these times you'll have the courage to finish what you start.' He came toward Alex, frowning menacingly. 'It's very interesting, the way you count on me to always be the gentleman. Well, I'm warning you right now, next time I won't.'

'There won't be a next time,' Alex retorted, scowling back at him. 'Just stay away from me.' She jerked away as Jake placed his hands on her shoulders. 'I mean it, Jake.'

'Oh, for God's sake, let's not fight. You're covered with hay. I was just going to brush you off.'

'No, let's do fight. It's safer,' Alex said, although how much safer was anyone's guess. That wild, dominating look in Jake's eyes excited her even when she did not feel his touch. 'Let's get out of here,' she said, wheeling about and starting for the ladder before Jake could decide that next time was going to be right now. She was not at all certain how much of a fight she could put up if he did.

The rest of the afternoon was tense at best. Every time Alex glanced at Jake she found him watching her, his eyes strangely glittering and thoughtful. She was sure she knew how a mouse must feel when it peeked out of its hole and confronted Murphy's huge, slanted green eyes, watching and waiting. But why was Jake watching her that way? Was it just that he found her unwillingness a challenge and was trying to figure out how to break her down? Or was there something else? Lorna? Peach Records? She did not understand.

Their trip home was conducted in almost total silence, except for the car radio, until Jake interrupted her musings as they drew near Central Park West. 'Well, shall I buy it?'

'What? Oh, the farm,' Alex said, trying to return to the more practical world from her futile attempts to comprehend Jake's alternating passionate and perfectly reasonable behaviour. 'I certainly would. That close to New York it's a good investment, even if Lorna doesn't like it.'

'You don't think she would?'

Alex shrugged. 'I don't even know the woman. How can I tell? All I know is she doesn't look the type who would enjoy puttering in a garden, barefoot and pregnant.' Her eyes grew wide as Jake threw back his head and roared with laughter.

'What's so funny?' she demanded, as a few minutes later Jake drew up in front of her apartment, still chuckling periodically.

'You are.' He turned toward her, smiling. 'Funny and adorable. Do you mind if we stop fighting long enough for me to tell you that I enjoyed today tremendously, in spite of everything?'

'I guess not,' Alex replied, wrinkling her nose at him. 'I enjoyed it too. Are you going to buy the farm?'

'Definitely,' Jake said with a positive nod. 'And there will definitely be some cows. I just hope they have better dispositions than you do. Otherwise, I may get kicked.'

Alex frowned. 'There is nothing wrong with my disposition.'

'See,' Jake said with a grin. 'That's just what I mean.' As he escorted Alex to her door he said, 'I'm afraid I won't see you again until Monday. I have a previous commitment to crew for some sailing races on Long Island, and you'd probably find it rather dull.'

'That's all right,' Alex said, although the idea of watching Jake sail did not sound dull at all. 'I need to get my thoughts organised before Monday anyway.' Last night, a glance at the printout the bright young man had given her had told her he was right. Lorna was no businesswoman. The whole complex report would need redoing.

Alex went into her bath and stepped into the shower, vigorously shampooing the remaining hay from her hair. Somehow she couldn't imagine Lorna tumbling around in the hay with Jake. Satin sheets and mirrored ceilings were more her style. It was going to be rather fun to turn in a negative report on her company. What could he possibly see in the woman? An interesting, attractive, exciting man with a brilliant mind deserved someone better. Someone more like...herself!

'Oh, snap out of it, Alexis!' she told herself crossly, turning on the cold water full force. She was beginning to put Jake and sex together in her thoughts far too much. And now she was sounding jealous besides! Well, that would stop right now. She had come to take a job and take on the challenge of working for Jake Jensen, not to fall under his spell. If she wasn't very careful, she was going to prove that what he said was right!

CHAPTER EIGHT

'WORKING already, dear?'

Alex looked up from the couch in the Dunsmoors' games room, which was only slightly less intimidatingly elegant than their salon. 'Oh! Hi, Mother. Yes, trying to decipher a code. I feel like a detective. You're looking sporty. What are you going to do today?'

'Peter's taking me to meet some friends on Long Island. He said we might go sailing, and I should dress accordingly. Do I look all right?'

'You look terrific,' Alex replied, smiling in spite of the twinge of envy she felt at her mother's announcement. At least one of them was going to get to go sailing today. In slacks and a bright, striped sweater, her mother could pass for thirty-five, and she told her so.

'Bless you,' Darlene said, looking pleased. 'Well, don't work too hard. I've got to go now. Peter's waiting downstairs. I'll see you this evening.'

'Have a good time,' Alex said, watching her go with a thoughtful frown. Peter Jensen was certainly showering Darlene with attention. She hoped it meant he was sincerely interested in her, and not just trying to distract himself from a still-burning desire for Lorna Beauregard. She sighed and shook her head. What on earth did those Jensens see in Lorna? There must be a lot more there than met the eye. Oh, well, she didn't have time to worry about that now. She had this blasted code to crack. If she could, it would certainly help establish her in the eyes of her staff.

The day passed slowly, Alex becoming more and more frustrated at her inability to decipher her predecessor's strange numbers. 'I give up, Murphy,' she finally told her furry friend, tossing a wad of scribbled-on paper for him to chase. 'I think you can make more sense out of it than I can.'

The loud chiming of the ornate French clock on the mantelpiece in the salon startled Alex into the realisation that it was very late and her mother had still not returned from her outing with Peter Jensen. What was that man doing with her mother all this time? His intentions had better be honourable! If Darlene wasn't home by one a.m.... Alex caught herself and smiled wryly. She was acting like a mother with a teenage daughter. Darlene could take care of herself. It was time for Alexis Faraday to go to bed, so she'd be ready to face a big day in the morning.

Alex got ready for bed, but could not sleep, repeatedly checking the lighted numerals on her clock radio. Where on earth was her mother? Could there have been an accident? If they had gone sailing, her mother wasn't much of a swimmer. Finally, she gave up trying to sleep and snapped on her light. The computer printout with its recalcitrant codes was lying on her bedside table, and she picked it up and glared at it.

'You *will* give up your secrets to me,' she said defiantly.

It was almost two a.m. when she heard footsteps in the hall, and there was a soft tap on her door.

'Come in,' she said, readying a smile. It died on her face when she saw her mother.

'What happened to you?' she cried. 'Your face is as red as a beet!'

'I'm sunburned. We were out on that blasted boat all afternoon,' Darlene replied. 'I must say it wasn't the most fun I've ever had.'

'What was wrong?' Alex asked, mystified.

'Well, Jake and that singer, Lorna Beauregard, were there too. Apparently, neither Jake nor Peter knew the other was going to be there, and they just glared at each other, but Lorna didn't seem to mind at all. At first, Jake was so busy helping to sail the boat that Lorna felt neglected, so she tried to latch on to Peter, who didn't seem to mind at all. I asked Peter what was going on, and he said he was only trying to show Jake what a fickle person Lorna is. Anyway, it only made things worse. Jake was furious. I've never seen a man so jealous. He dragged Lorna off somewhere, and he practically had a hammer-lock on her all evening. When Peter tried to dance with her, they almost came to blows. I told Peter I didn't think much of his baiting Jake like that, but he said he had it coming for being such a fool over that woman. I'm not sure I blame him. What on earth can Jake see in her? She's as artificial as a stuffed toy.'

'I don't know. Maybe she looks better horizontal,' Alex replied, trying to simultaneously quell the anxiety she felt at her mother's tale and hide the sudden fury that Darlene's account of Jake's jealousy produced. Peter Jensen was apparently not over his passion for Lorna, nor had he told Darlene how things had been between them. And the thought of Jake clutching at Lorna Beauregard made Alex feel like screaming and throwing things. Was the man out of his mind?

'No doubt,' Darlene said with a disgusted sniff. 'Anyway, Peter and I got things straightened out, but I won't see him all week. He and some cronies are going on their annual trip to some fancy fishing camp in

Canada. He'll be back for Jake's party, though. He says he'll go since I'll be there.'

And doubtless Lorna would, too, Alex thought wryly. She chewed her lip, trying to think of what she might say to Darlene that might hint of present and future problems.

'Are you really sure,' she asked finally, 'that Peter's being straight with you? Maybe he's really interested in Lorna, and that's why he and Jake aren't getting along.'

'Oh, all men go for that type,' Darlene said dismissively, 'but she's not the type that most men marry. She's a bed-hopper, or I miss my guess. I think that's why Peter's so upset that Jake may be planning to marry her. But if he intends to do any more demonstrating of her fickleness in front of me, he'd better watch out. And she had, too. I don't intend to let her get her claws into my Peter.'

Good heavens! Alex thought in surprise, she had never seen her mother sound that aggressive! 'Good luck,' she said with a smile, 'but don't get carried away. I don't want to be the daughter of an axe murderess.'

'I doubt I'll have to go that far,' Darlene replied with a confident smile. She glanced at Alex's clock. 'Goodness, dear, you should be asleep by now. Are you still working on that code?' She picked up the computer printout from Alex's lap and looked at it curiously.

'I'm afraid so,' Alex replied. 'It's got me stumped.'

Darlene looked at the page, then at Alex's bedside telephone, then back at the page. 'Why, dear, there's nothing to it,' she said, leaning forward and pointing to the letters on the phone dial. 'See? These numbers are 56762. That could spell Lorna, couldn't it? Is that the sort of thing you're looking for?'

Alex grabbed the paper and looked at it, and then at the phone again. 'Yes! And this one spells Peach! Oh, Mother, thank you! Thanks a million! You may have just saved me hundreds of hours of work! And when I think of all the dumb number series rules I tried . . .' She jumped up and gave her mother a huge hug. 'You're wonderful,' she said.

'So are you, dear,' Darlene replied, giving her daughter a kiss. 'But maybe sometimes you're too smart for your own good.'

Her mother was probably right about that, Alex thought as she switched off her light. After all, it was Lorna Beauregard who Jake had taken sailing, not Alexis Faraday. She frowned and punched her pillow. She was Jake's employee, not his girlfriend. She shouldn't care who he took sailing. But she did.

Alex found the next day that she had been correct in assuming her staff would be impressed that she had broken Mr Jackson's code. She hoped her mother would forgive her for taking the credit. She assigned two people to get the files printed out and bring them, along with summary statistics, to her by the next day.

'How's it going?' Jake asked, over the working lunch he had invited Alex to share in his office. 'Will there be any problem getting that report on Peach Records ready in time?'

'None at all,' Alex replied smoothly, even as she noticed that Jake had obviously got a little too much sun the previous day himself. 'Have a good time sailing yesterday?'

'Not especially,' Jake replied with a grimace. He slanted an eyebrow toward Alex. 'I'm sure your mother filled you in on the details.'

An uncomfortable flush started to come to Alex's cheeks, but she quelled it by fidgeting. Why should Jake look at her like that? She was only making conversation. Besides, it didn't matter to her if he wanted to make a fool of himself over that Beauregard woman. In fact, she'd rub it in a bit!

'She did mention that Lorna got a little out of hand,' Alex said, flicking a quick glance back at Jake, 'and that you practically manacled her when she did.'

Jake smiled wryly. 'I hope she appreciated my efforts. Tell her to hurry up and get a commitment out of Dad before I lose my touch.'

Alex's eyes widened. Was Jake actually afraid Lorna would go back to his father? Either the woman was insane or Jake was dragging his feet. 'Why don't you hurry up?' she suggested.

'I'm doing all I can,' Jake replied, sighing heavily. 'There are... things you don't understand.'

'Then explain them!' Alex exclaimed. 'I know Mother's fond of your father, but if she's going to have to compete with Lorna for ever, I can't see them getting together. I really can't.'

Jake was silent for a long time, staring at Alex thoughtfully. Finally he shook his head. 'I can't explain. Not yet. And I don't blame you for worrying about your mother. But Dad's really a great guy, and I think once he gets over this mid-life crisis, or whatever it is, he and Darlene will have a fine life together.'

'If Mother survives it,' Alex said drily. 'Well, thank you for lunch. I'd better get back to work.'

'I'm going to be out of town the rest of the week,' Jake said as he escorted Alex to the elevator. 'Paris and London. Think you can handle everything all right?'

Alex looked up at him. He was looking at her in that strange way again. She had heard it in his voice.

'Of course,' she replied. 'I'll be too busy to panic.'

'Good. If you need me, my secretary can tell you where to reach me. I'll call you, too.' He suddenly put a large hand across Alex's forehead, which was drawing into a frown. 'And don't tell me not to. I'm your boss. Remember?'

His wide mouth eased slowly into a smile, and Alex felt herself tremble from her forehead where his hand was touching, right down to her toes. She nodded.

'Yes, sir,' she said huskily. 'Have a nice trip.'

Jake shook his head. 'It will be thoroughly miserable. I hate to travel. I won't feel right again until Saturday. I'll be back in time to escort you and your mother to my party.'

Just before the elevator doors closed on Alex, Jake grabbed them and held them open and bent to give her a swift kiss on the lips. Startled, Alex could only stare as he grinned and winked at her before the doors fully closed.

What is wrong with that man? she wondered, bewildered. No wonder he couldn't get Lorna committed to him, as unpredictable as he was. Why had he kissed her like that? Did he really like her, as she sometimes felt, or was he just trying to annoy her? She shook her head, and returned to her desk. It was too much for her to fathom. She had that blasted Peach Records report to work on.

By Wednesday morning, the direction that report would take was clear. Judging from her preliminary figures, she wouldn't recommend that her worst enemy invest in Peach Records. She thought about warning Jake next time he called that he was going to have some bad news for his lady love, but decided against it. One never knew how secure the telephone lines might be, and he had been adamant about not letting any information leak out. She did hope he'd call, though. It was so good to hear his voice, and she wanted to thank him for the lovely little floral arrangement now brightening her desk. And, she thought with a smile, she wanted to tease him about sending them to all of the men at Jenstar, too.

'I usually send them a fifth of good whisky,' Jake growled in response, when she heard from him late that afternoon and told him, in as irate a voice as she could manage, that she was upset by the flowers. 'Would you prefer that?'

'Certainly not!' Alex replied, then burst out laughing. 'I was only teasing, Jake,' she said. 'I love the flowers. Thank you.'

'Crazy woman,' Jake said. 'How can you be such a good economist? I thought that was the dismal science.'

'What do you think drove me crazy?' Alex answered.

She was feeling positively light-hearted as she crossed the lobby of the Jenstar building to go out to her waiting limousine. She felt good about her job and the way she was getting into the swing of it, and she felt buoyed by the long conversation she'd had with Jake, who seemed more inclined to just talk than to be brisk and business-like. He did, she decided, really like her, and gave no sign of anything short of complete trust in her work. What more could she want? Well, if it came to that . . . She frowned to herself and halted her thoughts right there. Forget it, right now, she mentally scolded herself as she nodded to the doorman and stepped out into the slanting late sunshine.

'There she is!'

Alex turned her head at the sound of that phrase, and caught the glare of a flashbulb aimed straight at her.

'Miss Faraday? I wonder if I could have a few minutes of your time?' A dishevelled-looking little man in a wrinkled sports jacket hurried up to her, followed by another man carrying camera equipment.

'Who are you?' Alex asked warily. Was she about to be assaulted by one of those Press people Jake had mentioned? Apparently so, for the man pulled out a card and handed it to her.

'Mike Mulrooney, *Picto-News*,' he repeated the information on the card. 'I knew old Jake would pick a looker. How's he treating you?'

Alex frowned. 'I'm not sure I know what you mean,' she said, although she was afraid she did.

'Ah, come on,' Mulrooney said, with a loose-mouthed grin. 'I already checked and found out you'd been passed over for promotion at your last job, and it wasn't nearly as tough as the one you've got at Jenstar. What did you do to talk old Jake into taking you on?'

'I convinced him my last boss was guilty of blatant sex discrimination,' Alex replied, feeling her temper begin to simmer. 'Which he was. And I convinced him that I was capable of doing the job here, which I am. Now if you'll excuse me . . .' She started toward her car, where Jason was waiting, but Mulrooney moved in front of her.

'Don't rush off,' Mulrooney said, with another ugly smile. 'I'm real curious about how you convinced Jake you could handle the job at Jenstar. You must be some genius if you can make that company of Lorna Beauregard's look good, but I guess you've got to, huh? I mean, if you don't want to get fired like Jackson was.'

All of Alex's senses went on alert. 'No comment,' she replied coldly, turning and pushing her way past Mulrooney. He followed her.

'Look, Miss Faraday,' he said as he pursued her, 'I know Jensen must be pretty damn sure he can count on you. He's not gonna let Lorna get away just because her company's no bargain, and she won't marry him unless Jenstar buys it. She told me that herself. Old Jake must be doing something for you,' he leered suggestively, 'to make it worth your while to lie for him. And we all know what he's good at doing, don't we?'

Alex's temper went from simmer to boil, and she almost bit off the end of her tongue to keep from making some scathing reply. But she dared not. Quick thinking told her that anything she said could be interpreted in terms of the outcome of her pending report on Peach Records. Of course, she thought grimly, as she got into the car without saying another word, and Jason closed the door behind her, her silence could be interpreted as confirming Mulrooney's disgusting inferences. What a revolting little creep the man was, with his half-truths and innuendoes. Where had he got the idea that Jackson was fired for making a negative report on Lorna's company? That wasn't true. Maybe nothing he'd said was true. Maybe it wasn't even true that Lorna had said she wouldn't marry Jake unless Jenstar bought her company.

The rest of the drive home, Alex mulled over everything Mulrooney had said, trying to put it together with what she had learned from Jake. The conclusions she reached took all of the joy out of her day. Lorna had really made that condition, thus Jake's demand for total secrecy. He knew how bad the report would be, and he was afraid of losing Lorna. His only hope was to convince her to marry him before the board meeting. Thus his statement that he had until then to permanently 'prevent some damage'—Lorna's return to his father. How very strange. Peter Jensen apparently had a fascination for Lorna that Jake could only counteract with money. What on earth could it be? And poor Mr Jackson, her predecessor! He must have known the whole story and tried to help Jake's cause, getting the corporate axe for his trouble. What a sorry, complicated mess it was.

With a deep sigh, Alex got out of the limousine in front of the apartment building and gave Jason a weak smile.

'Tired, Miss Faraday?' Jason asked sympathetically.

Alex nodded. 'Very tired,' she replied. She was going to have a serious talk with her mother about Peter Jensen. It did not look as if he was the man for Darlene.

But Saturday morning came and her serious talk with Darlene had never materialised. She simply couldn't bring herself to put a damper on the happiness that shone in her mother's eyes at the huge bouquet of red roses that Peter Jensen had sent her. Why not hold out hope for just a little longer that things would work out in Darlene's favour? Maybe Peter Jensen was smarter than his son gave him credit for.

CHAPTER NINE

'ARE you ready, dear?'

'Yes, Mother, I'm ready,' Alex said for the tenth time. 'Do calm down. I'm sure Peter will think you look gorgeous.'

The two women were waiting in the Dunsmoors' sumptuous salon for Jake to come and escort them to his party. Darlene, her eyes bright and cheeks flushed, was looking unusually lovely in a gown of *café-au-lait* silk.

'I'm not worried about that,' she said impatiently, scanning her reflection in a gilt-framed mirror.

'Well, what is it, then?' Alex asked. 'Are you worried about Lorna Beauregard?' Perhaps her mother had heard the same gossip she had, she thought, her own forehead crinkling into a frown. It might be just as well if she had.

'No, of course not,' Darlene replied. She paused and nibbled on her lip. 'Well, sort of.'

'What do you mean?'

'It's just that...' Darlene stopped and took a deep, tremulous breath and then began again. 'I've done a lot of thinking this week, with Peter gone. If we go on seeing each other, I'd definitely like it to end in marriage this time. With all of the other men I've gone out with, I more or less knew it wouldn't last, but...I didn't feel about them the way I feel about Peter.'

'Oh.' Alex stared at her mother for a moment, and then went and put her arms around her. 'Oh, Mother,

I hope it works out for you if... if you really feel that way. You love him?'

Darlene nodded and smiled shyly. 'Yes, I do. And I don't want to do anything to spoil my chances, like throwing a jealous fit over Lorna. I think Peter may feel the same way about me, but I'm not sure yet. So, you see why I'm nervous?'

'I certainly do,' Alex replied. Drat Lorna Beauregard, anyway! If she could have one wish, it would be for that woman to disappear from the face of the earth. Her mother deserved to find happiness with the man she loved, not have to compete with that grasping bitch for his affections. 'I think you can count on Jake to keep Lorna occupied,' she said comfortingly. 'And if you feel like throwing something, just take a deep breath and count to ten.' Advice, she thought wryly, she ought to take to heart herself. Every time she even thought about Lorna, she felt like throwing things.

'Are you nervous too, dear?' her mother asked, seeing her anxious frown.

'A little. A lot of new people to meet, and all,' Alex said, smiling bravely. 'I'll be all right once we get going.' She, too, glanced in the mirror for reassurance. It was hard to recognise the sparkling, blonde beauty who looked back at her, the shimmering dress with its sequin-trimmed jacket setting off her colouring to perfection. That woman looked a lot more confident than Alex felt.

'Of course you will. No one's as smart and pretty as my daughter,' Darlene said encouragingly. 'Oh, good, I think he's here,' she added, as they heard the sound of Hawthorne's voice welcoming Mr Jensen.

'He is indeed,' Alex murmured, momentarily stunned at the sight of Jake in his tuxedo as he came strolling into the room. In the few days he had been gone, she had forgotten how the sight of him affected her, but her pulse had not and immediately started to race. There ought to be a law against a man looking so incredibly perfect!

'Good evening, ladies,' Jake said, bowing formally and then favouring them each with his warmest smile. 'I'd be the envy of every man at the party with either one of you, but with two...' he shook his head '...they're apt to accuse me of cornering the market on loveliness.'

'Cornering the market on blarney is more like it,' Alex said drily, trying unsuccessfully to calm her unruly senses.

'You should learn to accept a compliment more gracefully, Alexis,' Darlene chided gently. 'Besides, I'll take anything I can get from a man as handsome as Jake. You do look wonderful tonight, dear,' she said, going over to Jake and taking his arm. 'Perhaps we should leave my grumpy daughter at home.'

'In my Cinderella finery? Not a chance,' Alex said, quickly taking Jake's other arm, although she felt upstaged and even more tense at Darlene's apparently quick recovery from her own anxieties. She lifted her chin and looked at Jake, ready to thank him for his compliment, until their eyes met. Suddenly her mouth went dry and her mind went totally blank. He smiled slowly and she could feel her colour heightening and her heart pounding. Why couldn't she think of anything to say? What was happening to her? It was crazy! All she wanted was for him to kiss her again!

'Are you ready to slay some more dragons, fair lady?' he asked, his voice sounding to Alex's reeling senses like the purr of a lion who had just realised victory over his prey. 'I saw the papers. That was some job you did on Mulrooney.'

'Ready as I'll ever be,' she breathed, finally focusing back on the situation at hand. 'He pretty well slayed himself. He was so nasty that I just didn't say much.'

'I'll have to try that approach,' Jake said, with a mischievous wink that sent Alex's quivering nerves into another spasm. She was going to have to calm down or she'd never get through the evening, especially if Lorna was there.

Jake's limousine circled the block and drew up in front of his building with a flourish. A small group of people standing on the pavement immediately turned to stare.

'Reporters?' Alex asked, looking up at Jake.

'I'm afraid so,' he replied, 'but I doubt they'll be as bad as Mulrooney.'

'I hope not,' said Alex with a shudder.

They got out and the reporters zeroed in on their prey, peppering Alex with questions as Jake moved them toward the door.

'How does it feel to be the first woman executive at Jenstar?'

'Wonderful.'

'Do you feel comfortable working for a man with Mr Jensen's known attitude toward women?'

'Yes.'

'You don't care that he thinks there is only one position suitable for a woman?'

'He doesn't.'

'Do you feel Mr Jensen chose you because you are the best qualified, or because you're a woman and he wanted to pacify the feminists?'

'Both.'

'Beautiful,' Jake murmured, opening the door at last. He fended off the attempts to direct the questioning to him with a smile and a shake of his head. 'I think I'll let Miss Faraday do my talking for me from now on,' he said. 'She's much more tactful than I would be.'

'Thanks, anyway,' Alex said with a shudder when they were inside the quiet foyer, 'but I think I'll let you do your own talking. That's not much fun.'

'Are they always like that?' Darlene asked, wide-eyed. 'They're like a pack of wolves.'

'Only when they smell blood,' Jake replied with a grin. He gave Alex's elbow a little squeeze. 'I think Alexis successfully beat them back for a while, but they'll be back. It's part of the price of power.'

Power? Alex thought numbly. She hadn't thought of herself as being powerful. In fact, at the moment she felt about as powerful as a newborn kitten.

The elevator whisked them to the top of the building. The huge room, where Jake and Alex had shared such a quiet evening the week before, was filled with guests, the women sporting glittering jewels that Alex knew were not the paste kind she could afford. Alex had barely had time to catch her breath when Lorna Beauregard detached herself from a group of people and came floating toward them, her hands outstretched and her eyes glued to Jake's face as if he were the only person in the room.

Good lord, I wonder what holds that up? Alex thought, trying not to stare at the overwhelming amount of bosom displayed by Lorna's emerald gown which, where it did exist, clung like a second skin.

'Jake, dahlin',' Lorna cooed in an overdone Southern drawl as she drew near, 'give your Georgia Peach a great big kiss. It's been a long, lonely time.'

Georgia Peach? Alex thought wryly. So that was where that silly name came from. She watched coolly as Jake bent to comply. The woman had him absolutely mesmerised. It was beyond understanding.

'Lorna,' Jake said, ignoring Alex's lifted eyebrows as he straightened again, 'I believe you've met these ladies.'

'Yes, of course,' Lorna said, showing all of her pearl-white teeth and holding out a limp little white hand to each of them. She batted her eyelashes at Alex. 'How are y'all getting along with that little old report?'

'She's coming along fine,' Jake interceded before Alex could reply.

'*She* is also quite capable of speaking for herself,' Alex said, fixing Jake with an icy stare.

'Lorna, why don't you find Mrs Faraday a drink? I have to introduce Alex to someone,' he said, a sly little smile playing about his lips.

'Don't be gone long,' Lorna said with a sulky pout.

'I won't.' Jake winked at the tiny redhead and took Alex's arm again. 'Green doesn't become you,' he said softly in her ear.

Alex glared at him, wishing her cheeks would not turn red and give her away. 'Don't be ridiculous!' she snapped. 'I'm just not used to Southern belles. It must be an acquired taste.' She stared as Jake suddenly dropped her arm and pulled out his handkerchief, burying his face in it and coughing. 'Are you all right?' she asked anxiously.

'Fine. Never better,' he replied shortly, clearing his throat and dabbing at his eyes. 'But I'm going to get even by finding Ralph Grogan for you.'

'What do you mean, "get even"?' Alex demanded, frowning.

'Not a thing,' Jake replied, smiling blandly. 'Now, look your most charming, so Ralph won't think I'm a liar about how irresistible you are. I'm going to let him introduce you to the board members who are here. It will be less inhibiting to people if I'm not hovering around.'

And it will be less inhibiting to your getting back to your 'Georgia Peach' if you don't, Alex thought crossly, even as she smiled and shook Ralph Grogan's hand.

'Well, well, well! So you're the young lady who's responsible for my getting the shock of my life,' Ralph Grogan said as Jake departed, leaving them alone together. 'I can certainly see why.'

Ralph Grogan, Alex found, was a thoroughly charming, rotund man, who had taken Jake's bizarre behaviour with such great good humour that her embarrassment was quickly relieved. He led Alex from one group to another, helping to deflect tactless questions and filling in her knowledge about the board members with anecdotes that left her giggling helplessly. With one eye, she kept track of the fact that Lorna seemed attached to Jake like a green leech, and that her mother was in the company of a handsome, grey-haired man, who was unmistakably Peter Jensen. At least, she thought grimly, as her feet began to complain of what seemed like hours of standing, everything was more or less as it should be.

'I think you've done your duty,' Ralph said, as they moved away from still another group. 'How about some punch?'

'I'd love it,' Alex replied quickly. She felt more than ready to abandon the soda water she had drunk all evening, in favour of something stronger. On the way to the punch table, someone caught Ralph by the arm to ask him a question, but Alex continued on by herself. The punch table was near the windows, with a spectacular view of the lights of the city, and of the terrace, where several couples were dancing to music from a combo.

Alex picked up a cup of what turned out to be a slightly tart champagne punch, and gazed out at the dancers. Her hand stopped, the cup half-way to her mouth, at the sight of Peter Jensen dancing with Lorna Beauregard, and Jake approaching rapidly to cut in, a determined look on his face. Even from a distance she could see the two men bristle as the exchange took place, immediately remembering what her mother had said about Jake's jealousy. Judging from the look on Jake's face, she hadn't been exaggerating. But where was Darlene while Peter was up to those tricks? She scanned the room and finally spied her talking to Ralph Grogan, no apparent sign of distress on her face.

Thank goodness! She hadn't seen, Alex thought, relieved. She took a drink of her punch and turned her attention back to the dancers.

'Quite a bosom she's got, isn't it?' commented a woman standing next to Alex, also watching the dancers.

'Quite,' Alex agreed, wondering if Jake enjoyed having it pressed against his midsection.

'I wonder if it's worth fifty million dollars?' the woman mused aloud.

'Fifty million?' Alex almost choked on her drink.

'That's about what HP's worth. Funny neither he nor Jake can see it's only the money she's after.'

'It certainly is,' Alex said with feeling. Well, at least she now knew the source of Peter's fatal fascination for Lorna. His private fortune. She should have suspected as much.

It was ludicrous. How could Jake fall for anyone so blatantly obvious? How could Peter? She took a second cup of punch as other, more disturbing thoughts began crowding in. Peter Jensen probably knew as well as Jake did how the Peach Records report was likely to turn out. He was just dallying with her poor, innocent mother until after the board meeting, when Lorna would come scooting back to him. Meanwhile, poor Jake, obviously so smitten he couldn't think straight, was fighting a losing battle over a woman who got some kind of demented pleasure out of setting father and son at odds with each other.

She downed her second cup of punch and took a third, brooding about the misery that Lorna's vicious fickleness was going to bring to her mother and Jake. It wasn't fair. It wasn't fair at all.

'I think I'll just see what I can do,' she announced aloud to no one in particular. She set her cup down with a thump and began to make her way toward the dance-floor. She might not be able to change the outcome of that report, but Lorna didn't know that yet, and it might help Jake's cause if Lorna thought she had a little competition.

'Alexis, my dear, how are you? Sorry I'm so tardy in welcoming you to Jenstar.' Alex stopped and looked up as Peter Jensen appeared suddenly in front of her. 'You're almost as lovely as your mother. I can't tell you how delighted I am to have you on the Jenstar team.'

'Thank you, Mr Jensen,' Alex replied, trying to maintain an appearance of bland tactfulness in spite of the anger she was feeling about his duplicity toward her mother. 'It's going to be a challenge, but I'm looking forward to it.'

'I'm sure you'll handle it splendidly,' he said, with a smile loaded with the same lethal charm as Jake's. 'Your mother frequently tells me what an excellent head you have on those pretty shoulders. Which reminds me, where is your mother? I promised to take her on a buggy ride in the park.' He surveyed the room. 'Oh, there she is, talking to Ralph Grogan. If you'll excuse me...'

If he isn't a cool one, Alex thought, wishing there were some way to stop that little expedition without making a scene, and deciding that there was not. Who would ever guess what a two-faced snake he really was? The best she could do was pray that Darlene didn't take seriously anything that the older, but still devastatingly handsome, Jensen might say.

Alex went back to elbowing her way through the crowd and out on to the terrace where the orchestra was playing a slow tune and Jake and Lorna were still swaying back and forth, mostly in one spot. She came up behind Jake and tapped his shoulder firmly.

'Mind if I cut in?'

Jake looked around, startled. Lorna raised her head from Jake's chest, frowning.

'Oh, it's you,' she said, her arms still clasped tightly around Jake's neck. She tried to replace her frown with a smile, but her eyes impressed Alex as having all the warmth of a python's.

'Your favourite economic forecaster,' Alex said with an imitation of Lorna's fluttering eyelashes. She turned an adoring smile on Jake. 'You promised to dance with me, and I haven't seen you all evening. I got so lonely, I decided I'd just come and ask you. You don't mind, do you?'

Giving Alex a strange look, Jake detached Lorna's arms from around his neck. 'Run along and give Buster Llewellyn a thrill,' he suggested.

'Nevah! Ah'd as soon dance with a hog,' Lorna replied, her pout sulky to the point of ugliness before she caught herself and gave Alex another imitation of a smile. 'Have a nice dance with mah sugah,' she said before turning and marching stiffly away.

'What a sweetie,' Alex murmured, moving into Jake's arms. 'I can see why you can't resist her, *sugah*. You don't need to worry. Your dad's gone off for a buggy ride with my mother.'

'You've been drinking,' Jake said accusingly. 'And listening to gossip.'

'Only two cups of punch,' she retorted, frowning. 'Or was it three? And what I heard wasn't exactly gossip. Anyway, I know how you wish the Peach Records report was going to come out and why, and I'm here to help.'

Jake swore softly. 'Damn it, I thought I could count on you!'

'Shhh!' Alex pressed a finger against Jake's lips and smiled into his fierce glare. 'Look friendly. I'm not going to mess up the report, but it won't hurt if Lorna thinks I might. And it might help get her to make up her mind about you if she thought we had something going between us.' She stumbled slightly. 'Sorry. Two left feet.'

'Oh, Alex.' Jake sighed and shook his head. 'Why don't you just shut up and dance?' He pulled her close and laid his cheek against her hair, his hand firm and warm against her bare back. 'Tired?' he asked softly. 'This has been a tough night for you, between the reporters and meeting so many new people.'

'Don't try to change the subject,' Alex said, trying to ignore the sudden rush of warmth that Jake's closeness produced, and the feeling she had that she was melting into him. 'And don't get any wild ideas. I'm doing this for Mother, too. I think she's getting serious about your father.'

Jake chuckled and lowered his cheek against hers. 'That's good news,' he said, his breath whispering against her ear. 'But I don't think you can stop me from getting some wild ideas.'

Alex felt suddenly dizzy. Was it the champagne, or was it Jake? she wondered, clutching at him for support. 'Then I don't really think,' she said stiffly, trying to keep her mind on her original purpose, 'that I can help after all. You need to keep your mind on your goal. Or is that something you're just not capable of doing?'

'Could be,' Jake replied. He pulled his head back and smiled slowly, his eyes warm as a summer sky. 'Shall we have that as our song?' he asked as the orchestra, delving into their repertoire of golden oldies, began playing *That Old Black Magic*.

'Our song?' Alex said, looking away, and trying to still the erratic pounding of her heart. Damn Jake and those beautiful eyes of his! Black magic was certainly appropriate, but under the circumstances the idea certainly was not! 'I doubt that Lorna would appreciate that idea.'

'So?' Jake said with a little shrug.

'So you shouldn't be talking about "our song" with me or...or anyone else when your heart belongs to Lorna.'

'Who said it does?'

'You told me yourself that you stole dear Lorna from your father. I can hardly believe that you did it out of sheer meanness.' Aha! Alex thought. That had made Jake stiffen a bit. It must have struck home.

'I'd rather not discuss it.' Jake loosened his grip and fixed Alex with a forbidding frown.

'Well, that's too bad, because I want to,' she retorted, scowling back at him. 'That's my mother your father's got out in a hansom cab. I don't want to see her hurt, getting caught in the middle while Lorna tries to decide between you and your father.'

Jake's expression softened. 'Try not to worry.' He stopped dancing and led Alex over to the edge of the terrace. 'Please believe me,' he said very seriously, 'I'm going to do everything in my power to help your mother's cause.'

'Well, what about your cause?' Alex asked. 'If Lorna marries you, we wouldn't have to worry about either my mother or your father.'

She felt a wave of tension surge through her as suddenly Jake's eyes caught fire and flamed with a burning intensity. He cupped her chin between his fingers and tilted her face upwards.

'Do you really think I should marry her?' he asked softly.

'I...I...' Alex floundered, her throat going dry. As if hypnotised, she saw a vision within those pools of blue, of a scene that had such an incongruous aura of horror about it that a nauseating chill turned her hands clammy and her forehead cold and moist. Jake and Lorna, in full wedding regalia, were standing before a flower-banked altar. She saw the minister's lips form the words 'do you' as he looked at Jake, and then saw Jake's angular profile as he turned to look down at Lorna. A strangled sound emerged from her throat, as she quelled the urge to cry out 'No! No, Jake don't do it!' Within her chest her heart felt as if a dull knife were being twisted around and around inside it.

'What's wrong, Alex?' said Jake, bending toward her and letting his hand slide from her chin to rest along her cheek. 'You suddenly look pale. Don't you feel well?'

'I don't know,' she said, blinking rapidly as the intensely real vision shimmered and then faded. 'I feel so strange.' Why should imagining Jake marrying Lorna make her feel as if she were looking into a pit of the darkest despair? It wasn't a new idea. Why did it suddenly make her feel as if she had been condemned to some horrible fate? Nothing was different now, except...she couldn't stand it!

'Oh, dear God,' she muttered, as suddenly she understood. Jake's face was back in focus now, a small crease between his brows and a look of gentle concern in his eyes as he bent toward her. It can't be, she thought frantically, trying to deny the revelation. It just can't be! I can't be in love with him!

'Alex, tell me what's the matter? You're shaking,' Jake said, placing his hands lightly on her bare shoulders, an increasingly worried frown puckering his forehead as he studied her pale face.

Alex shook her head, backing quickly away from his touch. 'I...I don't feel very well. I think...I'd better go home now,' she stammered. She had to get away from Jake! Maybe it *was* some kind of black magic. Or maybe she had drunk more punch than she thought. Surely, when she could think clearly again, she would see things differently!

CHAPTER TEN

ALEX sat before the lavish, mirrored dressing-table in the bedroom of her borrowed apartment, methodically brushing her hair as she always did before going to bed, but hardly seeing her own pale face in the mirror. Images of the evening kept flashing before her, especially Jake's face, dark with self-disgust and contrition as he whisked her home, apologising profusely and sincerely for, as he said, 'asking too much of her for one night.'

'I ought to be horse-whipped,' he had said more than once, looking so thoroughly miserable that Alex wanted nothing so much as to put her arms around him, and comfort him and tell him that it wasn't his fault—she had been doing just fine until he'd asked her that one, simple little question. Instead she had sat stiffly in the circle of his arm, afraid to say anything lest she blurt out something foolish. She had wanted to answer his question then. She'd wanted to tell him that she certainly did mind if he married Lorna. She'd wanted to tell him that if he tried it she would tear him limb from limb, claw Lorna's eyes out, and throw seventeen kinds of screaming fits! In fact, she minded if he even looked at the woman! How she had managed to control herself when, as he bade her goodnight, he smiled that adorable, crooked, little-boy smile of his and asked, 'Forgive me?' she would never know.

'There's nothing to forgive,' she had answered him, only a slight quaver in her voice betraying her strain. 'I'll be fine in the morning.'

'You liar,' Alex said now to her reflection, setting her brush down and staring at her face as if it belonged to a stranger. That woman was not going to be all right in the morning. That woman felt all squishy and wobbly inside, and there was a huge, empty ache where her heart used to be. That woman had fallen desperately, hopelessly, in love with Jake Jensen. That woman hadn't learned a damned thing since she was fourteen! That woman was an idiot!

I can't let him find out, she thought grimly. I'll get over it. And I'll have to have a serious talk with Mother. The only safe thing for us to do is to steer clear of those Jensens and their little game of 'who's got Lorna now?'

There was a soft tapping at her door.

'Dear, are you still up? I can see a light.'

'Yes, Mother. Come on in.' Alex hurriedly pinched her cheeks to give them some colour and then picked up her brush again, pretending to be hard at work with it as her mother entered, still fully dressed, her eyes bright with happiness.

'Wasn't it a wonderful party?' she exclaimed, closing the door behind her. 'And the ride in the park was so romantic. I do adore Peter so. I don't think I've ever had a better time.' She sighed and leaned back against the door, her arms clasped around her.

'Yes, it was lovely,' Alex agreed, her heart sinking. How could she ever bear to snuff out that glow of happiness that lighted her mother's sweet face? 'I must admit, though, that I'm worn out,' she added, as Darlene frowned slightly after giving her a motherly scrutiny. 'It was a bit of an ordeal for me, you know, meeting all of those people for the first time.'

'I'm sure it was,' Darlene replied, 'but you were wonderful, especially with those reporters, and you certainly looked better than Lorna Beauregard. You should have heard what Peter said about that dress she almost had on. I really believe that Peter doesn't like her at all. I know he doesn't want Jake to marry her. He came right out and said he wished Jake would get interested in you instead.'

I'll just bet he would, Alex thought, trying not to appear as angry as she felt at hearing this latest confirmation of the duplicity of Peter Jensen. She eyed her mother speculatively and then sighed. Darlene probably wouldn't believe the truth if she told her.

'Well, maybe you can lure Jake away,' Darlene went on. 'You two certainly would make a gorgeous couple. Do you like him? It would be so fantastic—you and Jake, and me and Peter.'

'Mother...' Alex put her brush down again and shook her head '...I am here to do a job, not to chase my boss. And you can forget about any double weddings. I think Peter had better get used to the idea of having Lorna for a daughter-in-law. Jake as much as admitted that he's planning to marry her. He even asked me what I thought of the idea.'

'Oh, dear.' Darlene sighed heavily. 'I don't think I'll tell Peter that. It would upset him. Let Jake break that news to him when it happens. Well, I guess I'd better get to bed. Peter's taking me to a matinée concert tomorrow, and I don't want to look tired and wrinkled. Goodnight, dear.'

'Goodnight, Mother.'

Alex leaned her chin on her hand and stared at herself pensively in the mirror. Jake had said something about her being powerful, but she really had no power at all. Facts were facts, and she couldn't change them, in spite of the fact that the happiness of so many people hinged on that blasted Peach Records report. As a result, the two people dearest to her would soon be unhappy. If only she did have some power, preferably magical, she would wave her magic wand and turn Peach Records into the finest investment on earth. She made a terrible face at herself and then got up and started to turn down her bed.

'Move over, Murphy,' she said to the cat, who lay stretched out in blissful oblivion on the satin coverlet. When he did not move, she picked him up and hugged him against her cheek, grateful for his responsive purr. 'Oh, for the nice, simple life of a cat,' she said softly. 'Want to trade places with me?'

Her thoughts followed a similar line in the morning as she sat at the Duncan Phyfe dining-table, drinking coffee from an elegant silver service and looking at a newspaper's picture of herself frowning at a reporter's question. Meanwhile Murphy pranced daintily along the border of the deep red Kashan rug, pausing now and then to bat at a little silver ball which Hawthorne had found for him.

She startled and choked on her coffee at the sound of Jake's voice saying, 'Charming picture, isn't it?'

'Enough!' she cried, as he immediately jumped to pound on her back. 'Don't sneak up on me like that! Yes, I love the picture. I look like a shrew that needs taming with a whip and a chair. And don't say it captures the real me,' she added as Jake grinned and took a seat at the table.

'Would I say that?' Jake's eyes glinted with mischief.

'No doubt.' Alex looked at him briefly and then pretended great interest in her coffee cup. Lord, but he looked gorgeous in the morning, so fresh and vital.

'Would you like some coffee?' she asked, glancing up at him again. 'I'll get another cup.'

'I'd love some,' Jake replied. 'How are you feeling today? You still look a little pale.'

'I'm fine,' Alex said. At least, as fine as she was likely to be for some time, she thought, as she tried to endure Jake's scrutiny without giving any outward sign of the turmoil it created inside.

'I think you still need some extra rest,' Jake said, after completing a thorough survey of Alex's face. 'Take it easy this weekend. That's an order. You'll need all of your stamina for the Fosters' annual bash at Hyannisport next weekend.'

Alex made a face at him. 'I'll try,' she said. 'In between shopping and taking in some museums. Where are you off to in such a hurry?'

'We're closing on the farm this morning,' Jake replied, getting to his feet. 'I'm taking Lorna to see it this afternoon.'

'Good idea,' Alex said, although his words made the ache in her heart even worse. 'I think she ought to see it before you decide about any remodelling.'

Jake nodded. 'And, in line with your suggestion of last evening, I thought I'd mention how much you liked the place. I might even tell her that if she doesn't, I'll marry you instead.'

'Jake, no!' Alex cried. 'That's going too far! Lorna's apt to come after me with a gun if you say that. The idea was to only hint that something might be going on between us.'

She looked away in confusion as Jake smiled that slow, warm smile of his. Why, oh, why did he have to be so absolutely adorable? She started and looked back at him as he bent and brushed her cheek with his lips.

'I suppose you're right,' he murmured softly. 'Be good. I have to make a flying trip to England tomorrow, so I probably won't see you until Tuesday.'

Alex nodded, her eyes wide. Her heart was pounding so hard that she thought it would burst. 'Have a nice weekend,' she got out hoarsely.

When Jake had left she stared numbly into her coffee cup for a moment, then burst into tears. Whatever was she going to do, about both herself and that awful report? She would rather die than break Jake's heart! There must be some hope for Lorna's miserable company.

All through a Monday that seemed to stretch on for ever, Alex toiled over the Peach Record report, but at last she had to admit defeat. If there was any way in the world to make it even half-way positive, she would have found it. There was none. Peach Records was a complete lemon, in debt up to its corporate ears, behind on payments to its contract stars, and losing market share at a great rate. Compared to several other small record companies which Jenstar might acquire, it was the very worst.

Alex paced the floor of the Dunsmoors' apartment that evening, her head down, mentally visualising the assorted human catastrophes that were going to accompany the unveiling of her final report. She had never felt so helpless. For a time she thought of distorting the figures, but she knew she would be found out eventually anyway, and her precious integrity would be lost along with everything else. Most of all she dreaded showing the report to Jake. The board meeting was a week from Wednesday, a scant ten days off. Jake would be stoic, but she would be able to read the worry in his eyes as time closed in on him. Well, she wouldn't show him the report until he absolutely insisted on it.

Alex was sure Jake must not have any burning desire to see the final figures either, for he made no mention of the Peach Records report on Tuesday when he returned. Instead he invited her to dinner.

'Where's Lorna?' Alex asked.

'She's doing some concerts this week,' Jake replied. 'Why?'

'Why?' Alex shook her head. 'I don't understand you at all. It makes me uncomfortable, that's why.'

'And I don't understand you,' Jake said with a teasing little smile. 'I thought you wanted to play the other woman. I'm just giving you the perfect chance.'

'That was only when she's around to see,' Alex said tightly. Lord knew, it wasn't that she didn't want to go out with Jake. She wasn't sure she trusted herself to be the kind of sedate companion she should be under the circumstances. Of course, if they went to a public place, it might be all right. It would help keep Jake's mind off his troubles. 'Where were you thinking of going?' she asked. 'A restaurant?'

Jake's eyes twinkled. 'I can see that you don't trust me. All right, a restaurant it is, even though I'd prefer a quiet evening at home. There's a nice, romantic spot with wonderful French food not far from our apartments. Maybe we'll be in luck and someone will get a picture of us for the newspapers.'

'Oh, no,' Alex said firmly. 'Pick a nice, stodgy place where you might take a business associate. I don't need any questions about whether I've assumed a suitable position.' She blushed as Jake roared with laughter. 'I'm glad you think it's funny,' she grumbled.

'It isn't funny at all,' Jake said, suddenly serious. 'If there were any way I could stop that nonsense, I would. It's just that you're so perfectly honest and blunt, and I like it so much.'

Alex eyed him sceptically. Well, she thought, there must be some truth in what he said. He had taken that tomato in the face rather well!

Dinner invitations were forthcoming on Wednesday and Thursday nights as well, and Jake still made no enquiry about the Peach Records report. A fresh floral arrangement appeared on her desk on Friday morning. Alex began to wonder if she had misinterpreted Jake's intentions. He had been the perfect dinner companion, charming and attentive, and, although she'd often caught him looking at her with that peculiarly intense stare, he'd made no move to kiss her. Even though, she admitted to herself, she wouldn't have minded if he had. Was he perhaps still holding out some hope that she might be able to make Peach Records look to be at least a possible acquisition for Jenstar? She had been sure, when he had said that he thought he could count on her, that he meant count on her to be perfectly honest. But perhaps, with time running out, and Peter and her mother still not having reached any definite agreement, he was growing desperate. Love could do strange things to normally honest people. Perhaps she had better see if she could find out if he was getting any such ideas. When Jake stopped in her office to see if she had liked the flowers she decided to try.

'They're lovely,' she said. 'I'm going to miss getting them after this week, and I'm going to miss our dinners together, too.'

Jake frowned. 'What do you mean by that?'

Alex shrugged and looked away from his penetrating gaze. 'Just that, shortly after the board meeting, you'll be a married man, and it wouldn't be appropriate.'

'Oh, I will be, will I?'

There was a dangerously sharp edge to Jake's voice, and Alex glanced up again, to see him scowling darkly at her. He had obviously understood what she was driving at and was not pleased.

'I just meant that it's possible, isn't it?' she said hurriedly. Jake ignored her question.

'Let me see the Peach Records report, Alexis,' he demanded. 'Now!'

'Yes, sir,' she replied, fumbling in her desk for the hated document with trembling hands. She hadn't meant to make Jake angry! 'Here,' she said, handing it to him.

Jake flipped quickly through the document, so quickly that Alex couldn't imagine him knowing what was in it. After only a few minutes he flung it back down on her desk. 'Excellent,' he said. 'Don't change a word of it.' He moved back a few steps from her desk. 'Stand up,' he ordered.

'What for?' Alex put her hands on the arms of her chair, but did not stand, feeling a dizzying rush of adrenalin at the challenging glint in Jake's eyes. She shook her head, licking her lips nervously. What was he thinking of now?

'Alexis, stand up and come here.' Jake's voice was stern as he beckoned to her with one finger. 'Now!'

Like a puppet on a string, Alex stood and moved toward him, her eyes held by the deep lights within those magic pools of blue. 'What...what is it?' she said hoarsely, although the quivering in the pit of her stomach told her that part of her already knew. She stopped just in front of him and stood staring up at him.

'That's better,' Jake said gruffly. He put his hands gently on her shoulders, then slid them slowly behind her and pulled her toward him until her entire body was against his. Then one hand crept up beneath Alex's silky hair and cradled her back. 'Put your arms around me,' Jake whispered, dropping his head to nuzzle his lips against Alex's ear.

'You're...p-pouncing,' Alex stammered, even as two arms, which apparently had a will of their own, found their way around that strong, hard body and folded across the wide, muscular back.

'Only because you want me to,' Jake replied, rubbing his cheek against hers, then beginning near her ear to kiss his way toward her lips.

'No, I don't!' Alex cried, trying to keep some semblance of control over a situation that was rapidly getting out of hand. 'Jake, this is wrong. What about Lorna?' Just saying the name sent a cold dagger through her heart, which was racing madly now.

Jake laid one hand along Alex's cheek, repeatedly kissing her lips as he said, 'I'm...not married... I'm not...even engaged. There's...nothing morally wrong...with kissing me. So go ahead and kiss me...just the way you want to.'

With a little groan, Alex capitulated, her mouth seeking his as if she were starving for its touch. Ravenously her tongue sought the inner reaches of his mouth, while her body burrowed against his like a baby bird seeking the warmth of its nest. Nothing mattered, nothing existed but the two of them and their closeness. Jake's hand came between them and cupped her throbbing breasts, then delicately unfastened her blouse and slipped inside to massage the tender peaks until Alex uttered a shuddering sigh and dropped her head back, her eyes closed, the world whirling giddily about her.

Responding to her cue, Jake slipped her blouse from her shoulders, his lips seeking their rosy quarry, gently at first and then with such fervour that Alex gasped at the wildest sensations she had ever experienced. Don't ever stop, don't ever stop, was all that she could think as she clung to Jake's head and held it, her hands plunged deep in his thick, black hair. Then, very gradually, Jake pulled her back, his arms enfolding her again, his head resting against her hair. She stood in the circle of his arms, trembling and drenched with desire.

'Shall we go somewhere and find a bed?' Jake said softly.

Oh, God, Alex thought desperately, that was what she wanted more than anything in the world right now. But she couldn't. She just couldn't. She had no protection. She mustn't take that chance. Alex shook her head, looking up at Jake, her eyes pleading for understanding. 'Not now,' she said hoarsely. 'Maybe…some time soon?' She held her breath as Jake studied her. Why was he frowning like that?

'Some time soon,' Jake echoed. There was a strange hollowness to Jake's voice and a coldness to his eyes. 'And I suppose you're finally willing to make that concession in the interest of keeping your job with Jenstar?'

'Wh-what?' Alex stammered, staggering back as Jake thrust her from him. 'No! Of course not! Why do you say that?'

'You know damn well why I do,' Jake replied. With that, he turned and strode from the room, banging the door behind him.

For a moment Alex stood, staring after him. Then tears began to stream down her face, as she restored her clothing to its proper position with hands that shook so they scarcely functioned. Oh, dear heavens, she'd really done it now! Jake had felt accused of being unethical, of using her, and he had taken his revenge in the way that hurt the most. He had made her see exactly how it felt. And worst of all, he was so angry that he might never forgive her.

Alex tottered back to her chair, feeling weak all over, as if every bit of her energy had gone out of the door with Jake Jensen. How on earth was she going to survive the weekend? The next week? The rest of her life? It seemed she loved Jake more with every passing day, and now she had put herself in a position where she couldn't even try to help him and her mother with a little innocent flirting at the Fosters' party to try and make Lorna jealous. Oh, well, it probably wouldn't have worked anyway. She shuddered, and found a tissue to dab her eyes and cheeks. This time, she brooded, her mother had been wrong. Sometimes she was too dumb for anyone's good.

'Miss Faraday?' Alex's secretary poked her head in the door. 'Are you all right? You didn't answer your intercom.'

Alex stared at her. She must be losing her hearing along with her mind. 'I . . . I must have been thinking,' she said. 'What is it?'

'You have a staff meeting in two minutes.'

'Oh, lord! Thank you,' Alex said, shaking her head. How could she have forgotten that? She grabbed her notes and flew out of the door.

* * *

'Did you have a good week? I've hardly seen you at all.

You look tired,' Darlene commented as she and Alex breakfasted together on Saturday morning.

'It was busy,' Alex replied. She was not about to tell her mother that after yesterday she had written it off as the worst week in her life. 'How about you?'

'Quite nice. Peter and I have been doing the Metropolitan Museum, and he took me to meet some old friends of his over at Princeton University. Are you ready for the big party?'

'I guess so.' Alex picked listlessly at a Danish pastry. 'I'm not sure I'm looking forward to it.' As a matter of fact, every time she thought of it she felt sick to her stomach. She would gladly feign illness and stay home, if her mother wouldn't be so apt to insist on staying with her.

'Neither am I. I'd like it better if Lorna Beauregard didn't show up,' Darlene said, making a wry face. 'The wife of one of Peter's friends told me he almost married Lorna last spring. When I asked him about it later he said he's over her, but I felt better before I knew. I wish he'd told me before. He said he didn't because he didn't want me to think he was an old fool.'

'Oh, Mother, don't worry.' Alex laid her hand on her mothers arm. She had been so wrapped up in her own problems that she hadn't even noticed that Darlene looked pale and distraught. 'I'm sure Jake has Lorna well in hand.'

'Don't be too sure. I also heard Lorna has no intention of marrying Jake if Jenstar doesn't buy out her record company. I can't imagine anyone being that mercenary, but I guess it's not uncommon. Do you know how that's likely to go?'

Alex's heart sank. How she had hoped her mother wouldn't have to worry about that, too!

'I'm sorry, Mother,' she said, shaking her head, 'but I'm not at liberty to say anything about it.' She tried to maintain an expressionless façade, but her mother knew her too well.

'That bad, is it?' Darlene said with a heavy sigh. 'Well, I'll just have to hope that Peter really is over her, won't I? Even so, if she throws herself at him, with all that youth and glamour and bosom of hers, I'm not sure I can compete. I just wish she'd find some other man to go after. Some big Texas rancher would be more her style.'

'Damn that woman!' Alex burst out, suddenly furious at the agony Lorna Beauregard was causing her mother as well as Jake. There was no way she was going to let Lorna get away with making them both miserable without at least one more try to prevent it.

'Mother, perk up,' she scolded, clipping her mother's chin between her fingers and looking her squarely in the eyes. 'First of all, Lorna doesn't know yet how my report on her company is going to come out, so don't you breathe a word. Secondly, you get your act together and look your very best, and hang on to Peter for dear life at the party. It's supposed to be a romantic spot. Maybe he'll propose. Meanwhile, if Lorna's attention strays from Jake, I'll get it back there one way or another, or die trying.'

'What will you do?'

'Lord only knows,' Alex replied. 'I'll have to play it by ear.'

A continuous stream of elegant cars was discharging passengers when Alex arrived at the huge seaside mansion belonging to Merlin Foster, a member of the Jenstar board of directors.

'This is fantastic,' Alex said, dazzled, as Jason helped her from the car. She had never before seen a private home so large.

'It is indeed, miss,' Jason agreed, a warm smile briefly creasing his austere face.

Alex was shown to an attractive room decorated with flowery chintzes, and a lacy-curtained dormer window overlooking the manicured green lawn which swept from a wide, flagstoned terrace to the edge of the bay. The lawn was dotted with umbrellaed tables which looked like so many bright daisies from above, but the guests were standing about in little groups, as if they were not yet ready to lounge in the shade. One group of half a dozen people immediately caught Alex's eye. In it, the bright copper hair of Lorna Beauregard shone in the sunlight like a beacon, next to the white hair of Peter Jensen. She could also see her mother's blonde hair on the other side of Peter. But where was Jake? Alex squinted intently, finally picking out his black hair in a cluster of people close to the dock.

With a muttered oath, Alex flung her suitcase on to the bed and quickly pulled out her new sailing outfit. So it was happening already, she thought grimly. Well, she'd have to plunge right in and pray that Jake wasn't still so angry with her that he wouldn't speak to her at all. In minutes, she had changed her clothes, scurried down the stairs, and was hurrying toward the spot where her mother and her unwanted competition stood.

'Hi, Mother! Isn't this a lovely place?' she said, coming up beside Darlene and giving her a hug. 'Hello, Peter. Hello, Lorna. Good to see you. Has anyone seen Jake? I've got to find him.'

'He's over that way,' Lorna replied, gesturing toward the sea, a frown settling a crease between her brows. 'Why do you need to find him?'

Alex smiled sweetly. 'Just a little something I need to tell him,' she replied. 'See you all later.' With that she hurried off, a feeling of heat between her shoulderblades telling her that Lorna's eyes were following her. So far, so good. If only her heart would stop pounding and her hands wouldn't feel so clammy, she'd be fine. She could see Jake clearly now, and the sight of him in dark blue shorts and a white T-shirt nearly undid her. When he suddenly raised his head and looked straight at her, she thought she might faint.

'A lot of good that would do,' she muttered to herself, managing a weak smile and a wave instead.

Jake did not respond in kind, merely watching her soberly as she drew near, the fact that he did not look absolutely furious the only solace that Alex could find in his expression. He stepped back from the circle of people with whom he was conversing and waited, the way one eyebrow gradually slanted upward making Alex feel uncomfortably like she was going to be dealt with swiftly and then dismissed.

'Hello, Alexis,' he said when she reached his side, confirming her suspicions. He only called her Alexis when he was angry.

'Hello, Jake,' she replied, her voice almost failing her. 'How are you?'

'Fine,' he said tersely. 'Was there something you wanted?'

'Er...yes,' she answered, glancing back over her shoulder. As she had hoped, Lorna was not far behind. 'There's something I have to discuss with you.'

'Oh?' Jake raised both eyebrows.

Drat the man, Alex thought grimly. She had to think of something, and fast. She made a beckoning gesture and stood up on tiptoe, leaning toward him. As Jake bent his head, she whispered, 'I found some statistical errors in some of Jackson's other reports. We'd better go over them so I know if you want me to make some corrections before the board meeting. I brought the papers with me.' Out of the corner of her eye, Alex could see that Lorna was now upon them. She pulled back and resumed her normal voice. 'Why don't you come to my room later, and I'll show you?'

Jake looked at Alex through narrowed eyes, then at Lorna, whose sulky mouth was turned down as she glared at Alex. Obviously she had overheard Alex, and was not amused. Alex held her breath. How would Jake respond? Had she again been too obvious? He looked back at her, and she felt a rush of relief. The cold steeliness was gone from his eyes, although his expression was still carefully blank.

'I'll do that,' he replied. 'Perhaps after we're through sailing.'

'Wonderful,' Alex said, able to smile quite happily now. 'When are we going sailing?'

As if on cue, a hearty voice called out, 'Ahoy, all sailors! Let's get this show on the road.'

'I guess that means right now,' Jake said, giving Alex a little smile. 'Are you coming?' he asked Lorna, who was still staring coldly at Alex.

With a self-satisfied smirk, Lorna tossed her head defiantly at Alex and took a firm hold on Jake's arm. 'Of course, dahlin'. You know I love to watch you sail.'

Lorna tried to pull Jake swiftly away from Alex, who quickly took Jake's other arm. Lorna wasn't going to get her own way again that soon! She was going to make sure Lorna was really on her toes, for the entire weekend if necessary. She smiled demurely up at Jake, who had looked down at her in surprise as soon as he felt her hand.

'I'm anxious to see you sail, too,' she said. 'Of course,' she chattered on, 'I remember seeing you sail some small boats at Tamarack, years ago, but nothing as big as this.' She gestured toward the large yacht tied up at the dock. 'What do you call this kind of boat?'

There was a definite spark of amusement in Jake's voice as he answered, 'It's a yawl.'

'A yawl?' Alex giggled. 'That sounds like Lorna saying you all.' She glanced over at the other woman. 'I think it's so cute the way you do that,' she said innocently, her eyes wide as she looked back at Jake. 'Don't you think so?' she asked.

'Oh, yes,' Jake replied, but there was a strange note in his voice and, Alex thought, a very strange quirk to his mouth as he said so. He escorted the two women to comfortable seats. As Alex let go of his arm he bent swiftly and whispered in her ear, 'What the devil are you up to?'

'Up to?' Alex asked, wrinkling her forehead as if very perplexed at his question. 'Nothing. Nothing at all.'

Jake straightened and shook his head, his mouth twisted in a wry smile that clearly said he doubted her denial and, quite possibly, her sanity.

Once Jake had gone, Lorna got up from her seat next to Alex.

'Where are you going?' Alex asked quickly.

Lorna looked at her coldly. 'I'm going to the foredeck where I can see better. You stay right here. It's more comfortable.'

'Oh, no,' Alex replied. 'I want to see better, too.'

The look that Lorna gave her then, Alex mused, was definitely designed to kill. She had got under Lorna's skin and it was beginning to pay off. Now to see if she could keep her that agitated and live to tell about it!

Alex plonked herself down right next to Lorna's chosen spot, and for the next two hours chattered away to her, deftly turning away her frequent nasty or catty remarks as if they did not bother her at all, until Lorna looked, Alex thought with grim satisfaction, as if she might explode and start to burn around the edges like an overdone southern barbecue. She could not have borne it if it hadn't been for the pleasure of watching Jake, who was obviously an expert sailor. She wondered, with an ache in her heart, if Lorna experienced the same thrill that she did at the spare and graceful movements of his magnificent body. Whether she did or not, she certainly couldn't fault the woman for the undivided attention she was giving to him. Whenever Jake looked over at them, as he seemed to do quite often, Lorna would smile and wave, until Alex could barely resist slapping her hand. Jake, for his part, seemed quite entertained by it. He frequently smiled, his eyes taking in both of them with an amused expression that Alex could not interpret. At least he did not look angry with her any more. In fact, he seemed to be getting a lot more pleasure out of her conversation with Lorna than she was!

When the yacht had docked again, Lorna sprang immediately to Jake's side. 'Dahlin', you must be so tired,' she said, stroking his arm and tilting her face up toward him. 'Would you like to come to my room so that I can rub your back?'

In a pig's eye you'll take him to your room! Alex thought grimly. It's not going to be that easy. She took his other arm. 'Your poor back that you hurt skiing?' she clucked sympathetically. 'Does it hurt much? I could walk on it for you, like a geisha.'

This time Alex could tell that Jake was ready to explode with laughter. Instead he tucked an arm around each of them as they walked back toward the house. 'My back is just fine,' he said, looking back and forth between the two women, 'but you can't imagine how I appreciate your offers of help. Now, let's see. What games are there that three people can play?'

'I'm not in the mood for three-person games!' Lorna snapped, shaking off his arm suddenly and glaring at him.

'Neither am I,' Alex said quickly, sensing that Jake might be pushing Lorna a little too far. 'I'll just run along and leave you two lovebirds alone.'

'Aren't you forgetting something?' Jake asked, as she regretfully pulled herself free of his grasp. When Alex stared at him blankly he added, 'The papers?'

'Oh, yes! Well, they can wait a while if...'

'I think I'd better have a look as soon as possible. Why don't you bring them to my room in an hour? It's the last room in the south corridor.'

There was devilment in Jake's eyes now, and absolute murder in Lorna's.

'Yes, sir, I'll be there,' Alex replied, and made good her escape before anything further could happen. Jake had certainly caught on to what she was doing and joined in the plan with a vengeance! He had better be careful. Making Lorna a little jealous was one thing, but making her furious was another. She would have to speak to him about that. Meanwhile, she had a couple of other pressing problems to deal with. She would have to think up some good excuse for arriving at his room without any papers. That little spur-of-the-moment fiction was catching up with her already. And she had to steel herself for being alone with Jake again. It was getting harder by the moment to try to promote Lorna's cause instead of her own. Never in her life had she willingly given up to someone else on something she wanted as much as she wanted Jake. Especially since she was more and more convinced that she would make Jake much happier than Lorna ever could. If that were the only consideration...

'Did you have a nice sail, dear?'

Her mother's voice broke into her reverie and Alex turned to look at her. Her face was so sweet, so dear, so happy-looking now. She didn't deserve another terrible hurt. Yes, Alex thought, with a rush of loving warmth, for her I can do it.

CHAPTER ELEVEN

'HERE I am,' Alex said breathlessly, as Jake opened his door to her knock. She had half expected Lorna to be standing guard outside it, gun in hand. Instead, Lorna was nowhere in sight and Jake was standing before her, dressed only in his sailing shorts.

'Come in,' Jake said, standing aside and gesturing for her to enter.

Alex's second impression, after she had registered the contrast of Jake's very casual attire with her proper little sundress, was that Jake's room seemed almost filled by a very large bed. Her pulse started gyrating strangely, and she started at the sound of the door closing behind her, looking quickly up at Jake.

'Well,' he said, raising his eyebrows, 'where are the papers?'

'The papers,' Alex repeated, licking her lips nervously. 'Well, you see, I seem not to have them with me, after all. I thought I'd put them in the bottom of my suitcase, but when I went to look . . .' She faltered to a stop, averting her eyes from the penetrating gaze Jake had fixed on her. 'I'm sorry, I really did think . . . but I was in a hurry. I guess we'll have to wait until Monday. So I'd better go now, hadn't I?' She looked pleadingly back at Jake, praying that he wouldn't be angry with her again, and praying also that she could get out of his room before she was tempted to do anything foolish. Seeing him half-naked was sending messages through her that were anything but sensible. When Jake started to laugh she wasn't sure whether she was relieved or more unnerved than ever. She did so love the sound of his laughter.

'Is something funny?' she asked in a small voice.

Jake nodded. 'You are. I thought at the time that it was rather out of character for you to invite me to your room for a business conference, and it wasn't long before I realised that you were back to trying to make Lorna jealous. There never were any papers, were there?'

Alex blushed and looked down. 'No. Not here.' She slanted a glance back at Jake. 'But there really are some rather bad errors I need to show you on Monday.'

'Monday's soon enough,' Jake replied. 'Meanwhile, I told Lorna we'd be busy until dinner time, so here we are, with quite a bit of time on our hands. What shall we do?'

'Nothing. I mean, I'd better go. There's no point in making Lorna too angry with you. Is there?' Alex frowned as Jake shook his head, then turned around to the door behind him and locked it.

'I'll survive,' he said, turning back to face Alex. 'I think the first thing we'd better do is talk about what happened yesterday. Don't you agree?'

'Yes,' Alex said, trying to look down, but finding her chin lifted by Jake's fingers as he moved closer to her. His eyes had that intense look which she knew so well, and she found herself trembling, in spite of her intentions to face bravely the scolding she knew she deserved. 'I'm terribly sorry about...what I said,' she got out huskily. 'I didn't really believe you were only being nice to me because of the Peach Records report,' she went on as Jake continued to stare at her, 'but I was afraid if you had any idea how terrible it was going to be, and with time running out...I don't blame you at all for being angry with me.' She stopped, unable to continue, as Jake's gaze wandered to her lips and stayed there for what seemed like hours. 'Jake?' she finally croaked over the throbbing pulse in her throat.

He lifted his eyes to meet hers. 'I'm the one who should apologise,' he said, his voice as soft as the warm glow in his eyes. 'I know the pressure you've been under. It was inexcusable of me to fly off the handle like that. However, that isn't what I wanted to discuss.'

'It isn't?' Alex said numbly, mesmerised by the sensation she was having of slowly being drawn into those pools of deep blue, and the tingling that began spreading from the touch of Jake's hands on her shoulders.

Jake shook his head. 'No. I think the most important thing I heard yesterday was "some time soon".' He smiled crookedly. 'We seem to have a bed handy. Do you suppose that now is that some time soon? I'm still neither engaged nor married.'

Alex stared at him, thoughts running wildly through her mind. She should say no. She should get out of here as fast as possible. But...she couldn't. The door was locked. And anyway, she didn't want to. Not really. She wanted Jake, as much as he wanted her. She had for a long time. And this might be her only chance with him, one single, beautiful chance to know what it was like to make love to this man she loved so dearly. One blissful hour to remember for the rest of her life. This was no time to be timid and prudish. It was time to act on her feelings. She might not be experienced, but if the instincts that were telling her what she wanted to do were half as good at telling her how to do it, she would have no problem there.

Taking a deep breath, Alex smiled tremulously and nodded.

'You're sure?' Jake's eyes searched her face intently.

'Yes,' Alex breathed. A little shiver went through her at the touch of Jake's hands on her bare skin as his hands slid around to her back. Without another word, he took her into his arms.

The shock of Jake's lips meeting hers sent Alex's head reeling. If his kisses had been stimulating before, this was another dimension of such powerful and passionate hunger that it staggered her. It amazed her that she could respond in kind, searching his mouth with her tongue, eager to learn its secrets, to taste its very essence. He slid the straps of her sundress from her shoulders, unzipped the back and pushed it down. His hands slid slowly forward to cup and raise her breasts while his thumbs flicked back and forth over nipples that were inflamed with fiery sensations. Alex's head fell back and she gave a little sighing moan, her eyes opening to meet deep velvet blueness, dark and slumbrous with desire.

'Put your arms around my neck,' Jake said huskily. When Alex complied he lifted her, leaving her dress in a soft pile on the floor as he carried her to the bed. Carefully he set her on the edge, going down on one knee to remove her delicate sandals. 'There,' he murmured against Alex's ear as he gently laid her back on the bed. Nothing remained but her tiny, blue bikinis.

Jake glanced down at them, then back to meet Alex's eyes again with a bright glint of mischief. 'Lovely and lacy,' he said. He dropped a kiss on her tummy, his hand tickling along the edge of her lacy panties before he removed them.

'My turn,' Alex said boldly, as Jake crouched beside her, devouring her with his eyes. She reached out toward him, but he caught her hand and carried it to his lips.

'Don't be so impatient,' he said, stroking her with tender fingers. 'Let me enjoy just looking at you for a while.'

With a sigh Alex laid back, trembling beneath Jake's touch, her own eyes feasting on the strong, angular lines of his profile and the wide, muscular curves of his shoulders. She raised her hand and traced slowly down from his shoulder to his elbow, loving the solid strength beneath his smooth skin. Jake looked down at her and smiled.

'I'm glad you changed your mind,' he said, stretching out beside her and beginning to caress her hair back from her face with soft little strokes of his hand, 'but I wonder why you did. For a long time you seemed so sure you didn't want this to happen, in spite of how aroused you were. I want to be very sure you really want it now.'

Alex stared into Jake's eyes, her heart pounding harder than ever at the gentle warmth she saw there. Even now he was prepared to be the gentleman and let her change her mind again. To her, it seemed the only real question was why she had waited so long.

'I guess I just decided you were right,' she replied. 'We do want each other, and since you're not yet committed to anyone else, it isn't really wrong.' She let one finger follow the arch of Jake's dark brows. 'I'm not going to change my mind again,' she said softly.

Jake smiled broadly then and gave her a sudden, hard embrace.

'All right, as long as you're sure,' he said, getting to his knees and quickly removing his shorts. 'You can see the shape you've got me in already,' he said, with a sideways glance at Alex, who was staring at his male arousal, fascinated, signals of desire now stirring her entire body.

'I think I'm in the same condition,' she said breathlessly. Why did Jake still seem so reluctant? Perhaps he was still not sure how she felt. Perhaps he needed a convincing demonstration. 'Come here,' she said, taking hold of his arm and pulling him toward her with unmistakable intent, revelling in the feeling of his bare skin meeting hers. Eagerly she slid one hand behind his neck, bringing his head down until his lips met hers.

Jake's lips touched hers delicately, almost gingerly at first, but as her tongue flicked out to teasingly trace their lovely, sensuous curves he groaned and suddenly became as aggressive as before. Only this time it was so much better. The roughness of his chest caressed her nipples to a burning heat, and one long, hard leg was flung across her, so that she felt enclosed in his body, almost a part of him from head to toe. Behind her head, he plunged one hand into her hair; the other hand kneaded the softness of her buttocks. Against her abdomen she could feel his arousal growing harder and more demanding, pulsing movements beginning which she echoed as she felt a hollow need for him that became more insistent with every passing second. This was, she thought in wonder, the most amazing and beautiful combination of sensations that she had ever experienced. It was worth any amount of later pain to be here, now, with this special man, whose heart would never be hers, but whose passionate body would teach her things she would always remember.

Slowly Jake moved on top of her, and she knew that the moment when he would take her was at hand and that she would welcome it with all her heart. There could be nothing wrong with giving herself to the man she loved so deeply. Oh, Jake, she thought as he eased one leg between hers, I love you so.

Some time later, Alex wondered if she had actually said those words, rather than just thinking them, for suddenly something went terribly wrong. With an angry, growling sound Jake stiffened and pulled away, thrusting himself off her and into a sitting position beside her.

'Get up and get dressed,' he ordered gruffly. 'This is all wrong.'

'Wrong? What's wrong?' Alex cried, sitting up and staring at him, bewildered.

'You. Me. Here. Now. Everything.' Jake frowned, rubbing his forehead. 'It won't do. It's not right. It's not what you want. It's not what I want.'

Alex felt numb and slightly sick, her body in a turmoil of shock and frustration. 'What do you mean, it's not what I want?' she demanded. 'I wouldn't be here if it wasn't! Do you mean that you've changed your mind? You don't want me, after all? That's hard to believe, considering the last few minutes. In fact, considering what's been happening almost since I got to your room. What kind of weird game are you playing?'

'It's not a game,' Jake said tiredly. 'Just go.' He gave Alex a little push toward the edge of the bed.

Still not moving, Alex tried desperately to make some sense of his actions. 'You don't think I changed my mind just so I could write some "lady executive bares all" kind of article to prove you really do think there's only one position available for a woman, do you?'

'Good lord, no! Please, just get dressed.' Jake encouraged her departure with his hand again.

'Don't worry, I'm going,' she snapped, rage beginning to take over. She jumped up and reached for her panties and began putting them on as she continued in harsh, aggravated tones, 'But I really would like to understand your change of heart, if you actually have one of those organs. Have you abandoned your idea that two adults who want each other ought to go right ahead and have at it...' she jerked her sandals on one after the other '...as long as neither's really marched down the aisle yet? Or have you had a sudden attack of ethics? Does it suddenly occur to you...' she picked up her dress and stepped into it '...that maybe a man who plans to marry one woman ought not to go to bed with another?'

Jake sighed and shook his head as he watched Alex's contortions to reach her zipper. 'That's not it at all. Come here and let me help,' he said.

'No, thanks. I got it up once, and I can do it again. There.' Alex straightened, her hands on her hips, glaring at Jake. 'I don't think much of Lorna and I don't think much of you,' she said icily, 'but at least you two deserve each other.'

'Alex,' Jake said sternly, 'there are things you don't understand. I know you're upset and frustrated now, but please don't condemn me. When I can explain...'

'Forget it! *You* can't explain? *I* don't understand!' Alex said sharply, in a sarcastic sing-song. 'I'll just bet you can't. Well, let me tell you something you *can* understand, Mr Jake Jensen. You are to stay away from me from now on. Don't even touch me. Ever! I'll do my job and you do yours and that's it! One false move and I'll report you for sexual harassment.'

'Alex, for God's sake, calm down,' Jake said, standing up, still naked, and coming toward her. 'I should have made you take a cold shower with me.' He smiled gently. 'I know how frustrated you are...believe me.'

At the sight of that beautiful smile Alex felt her knees go rubbery and she began backing rapidly toward the door. What was wrong with her? Didn't she ever learn?

'Stay away from me,' she warned, reaching for the key behind her and turning it. 'Take your damned shower.' With that she turned and fled from the room, hurrying lest the sudden ache in her chest turn into an attack of tears she did not want to shed. Turning the corner into another corridor she almost bumped into Lorna Beauregard. She stopped.

'You'd better keep an eye on that man of yours,' she said to the startled woman. 'He's not to be trusted at all.' She hurried on to her own room without looking back, a lump that felt as large as a grapefruit in her throat by the time she reached it. She flung herself on her bed and buried her face in her pillow. The tears burst through, and for several minutes Alex cried like a baby. Then she thrust herself upright, dashing the tears from her cheeks with impatient fingers. She had asked for what had happened. She had known it wasn't something that would last. And maybe it had given Lorna the right message. Maybe now Jake could get her to say yes in time. If so, it was probably worth it. But why had he stopped like that? Could she have said out loud that she loved him? That might explain everything. He was too embarrassed to explain then that he had no intention of getting emotionally involved with her. Yes, that was probably it. Probably. Oh, if only she could remember for certain!

For the time that remained until dinner, Alex puttered listlessly about her room, not feeling up to talking to anyone. She thought of skipping dinner, but knew she could neither avoid Jake indefinitely, nor tolerate her own company if she turned coward and hid. Promptly at eight o'clock she appeared in the great hall of the Foster mansion, impeccably groomed, wearing her new gown of silver lamé, and carrying herself as proudly as if nothing at all were wrong. Only her mother might be able to guess that all was not as smooth as it appeared, but, to Alex's relief, Darlene was so wrapped up in Peter that she probably would not have noticed if Alex had turned green.

The dinner was very formal, the Waterford crystal, the Spode china, and the solid gold service impressive. The well trained servants were beyond reproach. Alex assumed that the dinner of roast duckling and wild rice tasted as good as it looked, but she had little appetite. She had to discipline herself not to stare at Jake, who was seated across the table from her. He looked so handsome, so completely relaxed and at ease, that she ached to go to him and fling herself into his arms. Love, she thought bitterly, was not as easy to turn off as sexual desire.

At the conclusion of the meal, Merlin Foster made a brief speech, thanking everyone for coming to make his annual summer celebration a success.

'And now, let the dancing begin,' he said, with a smile and a regal wave of his hand. The string quartet, which had accompanied the dinner with Mozart and Haydn, began to put away their instruments even as a small orchestra entered and began setting up, and the servants waited in readiness to remove the last vestiges of the meal and move the tables to the side of the immense hall. Alex drifted to a corner of the room, hoping to avoid both Jake and her mother. She was not sure she could endure dancing with Jake if he should ask her, and she had no desire to endure her mother's scrutiny, either.

Soon the music began, and Merlin Foster himself invited Alex for the first dance. After that, she changed partners with almost every dance, but Jake never approached her. Lorna apparently had taken her advice to heart and was clinging to him like glue. Darlene and Peter had disappeared, probably to wander in the elaborate gardens in the moonlight. Alex delivered a little prayer, in the hope that Peter Jensen would finally get the courage or inspiration to ask her mother to marry him. As if in answer, Peter appeared at her side just as she had finished a dance with a pleasant young man from the Jenstar computer division.

'Alexis,' he said, smiling at her warmly, 'would you come and have a drink with me? I have something important to tell you.'

Alex felt her heart turn over and her mouth go dry. Could it be? She nodded and smiled. 'Of course.' She felt as if time were standing still while she followed him to the bar and waited for what he would say. When he ordered champagne, her pulse began to quicken. At last he handed her a glass and raised his own.

'I'd like to propose a toast to your mother,' he said, 'the loveliest woman I've met since my dear wife died. She has just agreed to marry me, and I'd like to know that we have your blessing.'

'Oh, yes!' Alex cried, tears of happiness welling in her eyes. She touched her glass to Peter's, took one swallow, then flung her arms around him, suddenly sobbing uncontrollably. 'I'm so glad, so happy,' she said over and over.

'There, there,' Peter said, pulling out a handkerchief and ministering to Alex's tears with gentle dabs. 'I didn't know I was that much of a prize,' he added, with a mischievous twinkle very much like Jake's.

Alex gulped back her tears. 'It's just that I've known for some time how Mother felt about you,' she explained with an embarrassed little smile. 'By the way, where *is* Mother? Did she float right up to the sky when you asked her?'

Peter shook his head and chuckled. 'No, she's up in her room, packing. We're going to get away to some-place more private. She'll be down to say goodbye in a few minutes. Do you think your future stepbrother will be as pleased at our announcement?'

Stepbrother! Alex caught her breath, trying to calm the sudden panic that surged through her. Jake would be her stepbrother! How would he feel? Probably very relieved that Lorna no longer had the option of another Jensen.

'Yes, I think he will,' Alex finally answered.

'I think so, too.' Peter smiled wryly. 'The idiot has persisted in thinking I wanted Lorna back, without ever listening to what I might have to say. Shall we go and tell him?'

Alex felt her panic returning. 'Maybe you should do it without me,' she suggested. 'Lorna's with him, and she and I don't get along very well.'

'All the more reason for you to come along,' Peter said. He set his empty champagne glass down and bent his head close to Alex's ear. 'Your mother whispered to me about the Peach Records report, but, if that isn't enough to pry Lorna away from Jake, I'm making that your first assignment as my stepdaughter. You're to throw a monkey-wrench into that twosome one way or another, preferably by replacing Lorna. She wasn't suitable as my wife, and she certainly isn't suitable as Jake's, whereas...' he raised his head and gave Alex an appraising look, followed by a very warm smile '...you certainly are.'

'Thank you,' Alex said, smiling weakly. If this wasn't the strangest turnabout of all time! She had been labouring for days for exactly the opposite outcome, and now, at least as far as her mother was concerned, it made no difference. Somehow she didn't feel quite up to suddenly reversing her position, and she wasn't altogether sure that she should. 'Don't you think,' she said, as Peter Jensen began piloting her in the direction of Jake and Lorna, 'that Jake ought to be permitted to make his own choice?' She looked up as Peter made an impolite, snorting sound.

'I do not,' he replied firmly. 'The boy's out of his mind. He needs help. And if you're half as smart as your mother says you are, you're just the person to do it.'

As they approached Jake and Lorna, who were now standing and talking to another couple on the sidelines, Alex's mind was in a whirl that matched the spinning of her emotions. Should she do anything, as Peter suggested, if, indeed, anything needed doing? After all, Jake probably knew she loved him. What more could she do? There was still a good chance that Lorna would stick to her condition about Peach Records and Jenstar. The best plan, she decided, was to do nothing at all and see what happened after the report came out.

Peter walked briskly up to the two couples. 'Pardon us for interrupting,' he said, his voice very much that of the stern father about to take charge, 'but we need to talk to Jake and Lorna alone.'

The other couple politely disappeared into the crowd, while Jake and Lorna stared at Peter and Alex with widely disparate expressions. Jake looked alert and on-guard, while Lorna looked wide-eyed and confused. She, however, was the first to speak.

'Whatever is going on?' she asked. 'Is it something about the report on my company?'

Alex eyed her contemptuously, her temper instantly at the boiling point. 'Don't you ever think about anything but that miserable company of yours?' she snapped, voicing the first thought that entered her head.

'Alexis!' Jake said warningly.

'Oh, be quiet, Jake,' Alex said, turning her glare on him. 'She deserves to know exactly where her company stands, which is nowhere, and you deserve to hear exactly what I think of a man who would fall for anyone as selfish and mercenary as she is. Not very much! But that is neither here nor there. Your father has something much more important to tell you.' She looked up at Peter, who was watching and listening with a wide grin. He now rubbed his chin and turned his attention to Jake.

'I've just taken the first step toward acquiring this outspoken young lady as your stepsister,' he said. 'I'm going to marry her mother.'

Alex thought that she had never before seen anything as beautiful as the transformation that came over Jake's face. Tears sprang to his eyes, a smile of radiant happiness lighting his face. Wordlessly, the two men embraced. When Alex looked down again, Lorna was gone. Not such a bad move, she thought, glancing again at the two men, who were now beginning to talk to each other at a great rate. This was a good time for her to seek out her mother and congratulate her.

As Alex climbed the staircase to her mother's room, the magnitude of her outspokenness suddenly hit her, and she felt almost sick. Drat that Lorna again! She had felt so angry at Lorna's endless concern over that blasted company of hers that she had completely forgotten her own resolution of only minutes before to let well enough alone until the report came out publicly. Not only that, but she had insulted Lorna in front of Jake, which would probably only serve to drive him to her defence, and she had insulted Jake himself! How utterly tactless and stupid she had been! Now, when she even had Peter Jensen's blessing for taking Jake away from Lorna, she had done exactly the wrong things. If Lorna refused to marry him, Jake would probably now be so angry and bitter that Alexis Faraday would be lucky to keep her job with Jenstar, let alone get close again to her boss, the man she loved so deeply.

At her mother's door, Alex paused and rearranged her anguished features. This was no time for regrets. This was a time for joy. At least one of the outcomes she had prayed for had actually come to pass. She tapped firmly on the door, and when her mother appeared, she flung her arms around her.

'Mother, congratulations,' she cried. 'I'm so happy for you. Peter just told me.'

Darlene Faraday was, indeed, almost cloud high with happiness. 'Isn't it wonderful?' she replied. 'Peter said he was going to wait until he had the ring, but he decided he couldn't stand it any longer. He was afraid some other man might come along and sweep me off my feet. Can you imagine? I told him that would never happen. I think I may let him talk me into going to Las Vegas for a quick wedding, though. I don't want a big fuss, and I'll be very happy to have it all official. Now, how soon are you going to take Jake away from that dreadful Beauregard woman?'

'You, too?' Alex said with a sigh. 'Probably never. We fight half of the time. I think brother and sister is much more appropriate for us.'

'Nonsense,' Darlene said sharply. 'I've seen him look at you and I've seen you look at him. The only problem is that you aren't doing it at the same time.'

Oh, how I wish it were that simple, Alex thought, giving her mother a smile and a hug. 'I'll see what I can do,' she said. 'Meanwhile, you and Peter have a wonderful time. And let me know if you decide to dash off to Las Vegas, so I won't worry.'

'Of course, dear. Good luck with Jake.' Darlene smiled suddenly. 'Why don't you tell him you're applying for a more suitable position?'

CHAPTER TWELVE

ALEX did not return to the dance. Early the next morning she called for Jason and her limousine, and drove back to New York City. It was far better, she felt, to leave Jake alone to cope with Lorna. She doubted her meddling had had much influence on her mother's successful romance. Peter Jensen was apparently not nearly as foolish as Jake had thought him. And she had probably only made things worse for Jake. The last thing in the world she needed was to see those beautiful blue eyes staring at her accusingly.

That night Darlene called from Las Vegas. She was now Mrs Peter Jensen. 'We'll be back in time for the board meeting on Wednesday,' she said, that remark casting a pall over the brief lift in spirits which hearing her mother's happy voice had afforded Alex. The Jenstar board meeting was not on the list of things Alex was looking forward to with any pleasure.

On Monday morning, Alex felt as jolly as a prisoner on Death Row, waiting for Jake to call her and ask to see the information she had prepared on errors in her predecessor's reports. No call was forthcoming. After lunch Jake's secretary called.

'Would you send up a copy of the Peach Records report, and the additional information you have on Mr Jackson's statistical problems?' she asked courteously. 'Mr Jensen won't be in today. I'm to drop them off at his apartment later.'

'Of course,' Alex replied, her heart sinking even further. Jake didn't even want to see her. Oh, why hadn't she kept her ill-tempered mouth shut? She sent off the papers and spent the rest of the day trying desperately to focus her attention on preparing her own presentation to the board meeting, which was now only two days away.

On Tuesday morning, groggy from a night of poor sleep, Alex got out of her car in front of the Jenstar building to see the rumpled little figure of Mike Mulrooney, the reporter, hovering by the door. Wondering grimly what kind of dirt he was digging in now, Alex steeled herself to be impassive no matter what he said.

'Good morning, Miss Faraday,' he said cheerily as she drew near. 'I was hoping to see you. Got a couple of questions I'd like to ask.'

'I'm not sure I have any answers,' Alex replied with a tired sigh.

'Finding the new job kind of tough?' Mulrooney asked, immediately noticing her indication of fatigue.

Alex snapped herself to attention and glared at him coldly. 'If you're asking if it's too much for me, the answer is no,' she said. 'It's going very well.'

Mulrooney grinned. 'Don't worry, I'm not out to get you. I heard you were doing real well. What I wanted to ask is if you might know who it is your boss is marrying. He stopped in Tiffany's yesterday and bought a big diamond ring, but it isn't for Lorna Beauregard.'

A riffle of nervous tension went through Alex's body. Jake had bought a diamond? 'But it must be!' she blurted. 'What makes you think it isn't?'

'I asked the lady,' Mulrooney replied. 'From what she said, she and Jensen are all washed up. In fact, she was pretty graphic about what she thinks of him, if you know what I mean.'

'Oh, my,' Alex said, her mind reeling at this revelation. She shook her head. 'Really, Mr Mulrooney, I don't know of anyone else. Mr Jensen's never mentioned anyone to me. Perhaps he still hopes to win Miss Beauregard back.'

'I don't think so,' Mulrooney said, frowning. He eyed Alex speculatively. 'It couldn't be you, could it?'

'Good heavens, no!' Alex cried. 'He's my boss and I'm his employee.' All she needed was for Jake to think she'd led this miserable gossip-monger to that conclusion.

'Well, there must be someone who likes country living in line for the job,' Mulrooney said. 'I hear he's got a regular army working at that farm he bought in Connecticut, getting it all fixed up, like he's planning to go there with someone real soon. Now, I'm sure it's a fine place, but it's not exactly Lorna's cup of tea. She may sing country, but she's more into high living in the city. I don't think takin' her off to a farm would score many points.'

'I suppose not.' Alex shook her head again, totally unable to comprehend this latest turn of events. 'I'm sorry, Mr Mulrooney, but I'm afraid this is all as big a mystery to me as it is to you. Maybe bigger. You probably know a lot more about the other women Mr Jensen has been involved with than I do.'

Mulrooney shrugged. 'Thanks, anyway, Miss Faraday. I just thought maybe, since you're a woman, you might have heard something interesting. Well, have a nice day.'

'Same to you,' Alex replied, still so stunned that she almost walked into the door before the doorman could open it for her. What an utterly amazing and unpredictable man Jake Jensen was! The way he had pursued

Lorna Beauregard, she would have thought he would
have been heartbroken if she really decided not to marry
him. But maybe, since he knew all along it was a possibility, he had been braced for it, and had someone else
in mind to replace her in his affections. Perhaps there
was another woman, just waiting in the wings, praying
he would get tired of Lorna and come back to her.

'I don't know whether I'm glad or sorry,' Alex murmured to herself as she sat down at her desk and leaned
her chin on her hand. In a way, she was glad that Jake
was apparently going on with his life without Lorna. He
wouldn't be so angry with her, then. But this time, it
looked as if he would be closing her out of his life for
ever, and very soon. A tear trickled out of her eye and
down to her chin. Who was she kidding? She wasn't the
least bit glad. Not really! She hated whoever this new
woman was with a passion. It wasn't fair! Why hadn't
Jake given Alexis Faraday a chance? Wasn't there anything she could do to make him think of her that way
before it was too late? There must be. This time she
wasn't going to give up willingly!

Alex gnawed on her knuckles and stared into space.
What could she do? Jake already knew she was physically attracted to him. He might even know that she loved
him, although he may have discounted that as having
been said at the height of passion. He didn't, however,
know that she wanted to marry him. Apply for the position, her mother had said. Hmmm, that might be an
idea. It was a long shot, and Jake might be embarrassed
at having to turn her down, but after all the heartache
he had caused her she wasn't going to worry too much
about that. At least it would call attention to the fact
that she was available. After all, a woman couldn't very
well expect to get a job if no one knew she wanted it.

An hour later, her 'application' completed, Alex called Jake's office.

'Is Mr Jensen in today?' she asked.

'No, Miss Faraday, he isn't,' the secretary answered. 'He's at his farm, tending to some details of the renovation. He said to expect him back first thing tomorrow, though.'

'Good,' Alex replied. 'I have something for him. I'll bring it right up.' She had hoped he was away, so that she could leave the application, sealed tightly in an envelope marked 'Personal' in red letters, on his desk without encountering him. She did so just before going home, and then left Jenstar with her nerves drawn tight as bowstrings. Jake would doubtless see the letter in the morning before the board meeting, but he wouldn't have time to say anything to her until afterwards. That would give him some time to recover from the shock. Whether she would recover, she was not sure.

In the morning, Alex spent extra time on her appearance. She had a new suit of natural raw silk, a pale blue silk blouse, and black patent pumps. The perfect young executive, she congratulated herself as she gazed into the mirror. Too bad it might not look to Jake like the perfect wife. She bent forward and surveyed her face critically. Thanks to cosmetics, the pallor of nervousness was well hidden, and her unnaturally bright eyes only looked as if she had been very clever with her make-up.

'Why can't I be as naturally gorgeous as you?' she said to Murphy, who was rubbing happily around her legs. She picked him up and bumped her nose against his pink one briefly. 'Wish me luck with Jake, old friend,' she told him, returning his green-eyed stare with a blue-eyed one. 'You might end up on a farm where there are lots of mice to catch. Think you'd like that?'

'Yow,' Murphy replied grumpily, wriggling to be put down.

'I think you're getting spoiled,' Alex told him, with a wry smile. Hawthorne, she knew, treated him like royalty.

Alex went directly to her office when she reached the Jenstar building. Her presentation to the board was scheduled for eleven o'clock, and she did not want to go to the executive suite until just before that time. She left word that she was not to be disturbed for any reason, and spent the time going over her material until she was sure she was letter perfect. At ten minutes to eleven she got into the elevator, perfectly calm about meeting the board of directors of one of the world's largest corporations, but tied in a thousand knots over seeing its president and chief executive officer again. She was sure she would be able to tell by the look on Jake's face what his response to her application was going to be.

At precisely eleven o'clock, Jake emerged from the conference room and greeted her warmly. There was an aura of tension about him, and his eyes seemed to glow with some inner light, but Alex could not, for the life of her, decide what those symptoms meant in terms of her letter to him.

'Nervous?' he asked her quietly, taking her arm.

'Not very,' she lied. Seeing Jake again had destroyed what semblance of calm she had had only a few minutes before. She knew it would take all of her resources to concentrate on doing justice to her presentation. When he smiled slowly at her, she thought wildly for a moment of letting out a piercing scream and running for the fire exit, but she regained her control and went with Jake into the conference room, smiling pleasantly as he introduced her to the assembled group. She took her place at the end of the long table, standing before some displays she had prepared, and launched into her talk. Her nervousness disappeared as she discussed the carefully analysed data, and answered the questions of the board members. It was only a few minutes before noon when she finished, to the approving applause of the board.

'An excellent presentation, Miss Faraday,' Jake said. 'Thank you. We'll adjourn for luncheon now. My father will chair the afternoon meeting. Miss Faraday, if you would come with me, please?'

Jake raised his eyebrows questioningly at Alex, whose stomach quickly turned into a knotted mass. She was about to find out exactly what Jake thought of her application, and suddenly she wished desperately that she had never made it. He must have thought she was crazy! Trembling with dread, she followed the board members from the room, and then let Jake lead her into his office. He pulled a chair over to a position next to his. When Alex only stood numbly beside it, he nodded toward the chair.

'I think maybe you'd better sit down,' he said, a wry little smile playing about his lips.

Alex nodded and sat, but as she did she glanced at Jake's desk. Her letter was still lying there, unopened! Beside it was a folded-open copy of the daily *Picto-News*.

'Alexis,' Jake said, sitting down and beginning to tap the ends of his fingers together, 'sometimes I think I should have given you an intelligence test before I offered you a job at Jenstar.'

'You what?' Alex cried, jerking her attention back to Jake.

'I said...' Jake began.

'I know. I heard you,' Alex said, her eyes drifting back to the letter. She had suddenly, chillingly, realised that what Jake was about to say to her was related to whomever he had bought the ring for. He had no idea what was in her letter. She had to get it back before he did!

'I read Mulrooney's column this morning,' Jake went on. 'It seems he talked to you yesterday.'

'Yes, he did,' Alex said hurriedly. 'Jake . . . that letter on your desk. I want it back. Please.'

'What letter?' Jake turned toward his desk and picked it up. 'Oh, is this from you?' He looked from it to Alex's taut expression and then back at the letter. 'Why do you want it back? It says "Personal". That makes me very curious.' He held the letter up and squinted at it. 'I wonder what's inside?'

'Jake, please,' Alex said, reaching for the letter. 'It's something I don't want you to see now. It might be very embarrassing for both of us.'

'Embarrassing?' Jake made a comical face. 'What about this?' He picked up the newspaper with his other hand and waved it toward her.

'I don't see that that's embarrassing at all,' Alex snapped, making a lunge for the letter in Jake's right hand. 'I only told the truth. *Please* give me my letter.'

'Oh, no,' Jake said, standing and holding the letter over his head, while Alex tried vainly to reach it. 'And while you're chasing the letter, please try to explain to me why you told Mulrooney that you have no idea who I'm planning to marry and why you thought I was idiot enough to buy a ring for Lorna Beauregard.'

'Because I don't know!' Alex said in anguished tones, pursuing the letter as Jake changed hands behind his back. 'I thought you loved Lorna.' She made a small jump and caught Jake's arm, dragging it down to where she could get a grip on the letter. 'Let go!' she commanded, frustrated at the strength of his hold.

'Not on your life. What's in there must be more intelligent than what you told Mulrooney. Did you finally hazard a guess at who it might be?'

'Certainly not!' Alex denied, although she had told him who it should be, and the closeness of his guess made her flush uncomfortably. 'Now give it to me or I'll...I'll bite!'

At that, Jake roared with laughter and finally released the letter. 'I can't go through that again,' he said, chuckling still. 'There's no lake to throw you in. Now sit down and listen to me.'

'Yes, sir,' Alex said, placing the letter on the seat of her chair and then sitting on it for safety. 'All right,' she said, knotting her hands together in her lap to stop their obvious shaking, 'tell me who it is, since I'm so stupid. That's what you brought me in here for, isn't it?'

Jake nodded, leaning back in his chair and rubbing his thumb thoughtfully across his chin, staring at Alex intently all the while.

'You've made this rather difficult for me,' he said, smiling crookedly. 'I had planned something more elegant.'

'Elegant?' Alex's voice was thin and she felt strange stirrings at the intensity with which Jake was staring at her. She could not have torn her eyes from his if she tried.

'Yes,' Jake replied. He sat forward. 'Well, why not pretend to do it the way I planned? Imagine, if you will, a beautiful room full of flowers.' He made a sweeping gesture with one hand. 'We have just finished a lovely dinner. Musicians are playing something by Mozart. You are dressed in a beautiful gown, sitting on a velvet chair. I come to you and go down on bended knee...' he proceeded to do so '...and take your hands in mine.' He took Alex's chilly fingers into his large, warm hands. 'Lovely lady, I say, I hope that you will look upon the suit of this humble servant with favour. I know these past weeks have been difficult for you, as they have for me, but I hold out some hope that deep in your heart you feel some small semblance of the love I feel for you. If you do, please take this as a token of my love...' he pulled a ring from his pocket and slowly slid it on Alex's finger '...and make me the happiest man on earth by agreeing to become my wife.' Jake then carried Alex's hand to his lips, but all the while his eyes never left her face.

Alex, for her part, was so shaken she was unable to speak. Her lips were parted, and a mist seemed to have formed before her eyes. She could not believe that what she had just seen and heard was really happening. At last she whispered hoarsely, 'I'm dreaming. Things like this...don't really happen.'

'Yes, they do,' Jake said, standing and pulling her to her feet and into his arms. 'If you wish hard enough. That was a yes, wasn't it?'

The solid, warm strength of Jake's arms around her finally penetrated through the fog of Alex's confusion. It was real! Jake had just asked her to marry him!

'Yes!' she cried happily. 'Oh, yes, of course I'll marry you.' She flung her arms around him, buried her cheek against his neck, and burst into tears of relief and joy. 'I'm sorry,' she gasped, trying to force down the tears, her mind still unable to fully grasp what had happened, but her heart already full of a growing warmth as she clung to Jake for strength in a world that had suddenly been turned upside down. She looked up, dizzy with happiness at the love she saw now in Jake's eyes, but with unanswered questions flying through her mind in a confused jumble.

'Why,' she complained, when she could find her voice, 'didn't you tell me before? Why did you let me think you cared for Lorna? Couldn't you see that I loved you, too, and you were breaking my heart?' She pulled her head back, staring into the beautiful blue eyes, so full of love, and then shook her head. 'Never mind,' she said softly, 'just kiss me. It doesn't matter any more.'

Jake's lips curved into an adoring smile. 'I'll explain it all, but I think we should do some serious lovemaking first. I want you so much I'm about to explode. See?' He took Alex's hand and held it against him.

'Me, too,' she whispered, caressing him and feeling the terrible ache that had filled her whole body for so long suddenly become focused into a hungry yearning for the kind of fulfilment that she knew was no longer going to be denied her. 'But it's a terribly long way to your apartment.'

'Just come with me,' Jake said, sweeping her into his arms. He went to a bookcase on the side wall of his office and pressed a series of numbers on what looked like a tiny computer. A part of the wall slid open to reveal a complete, luxurious bedroom. 'Every real executive suite has one,' Jake said, grinning at Alex's amazed stare. He carried her through the doorway and turned to press another series of buttons. 'And no one else knows the combination,' he said, with a wicked wink that made Alex giggle delightedly as the door slid closed behind them.

'I expect we may get quite a bit of use out of this room from now on,' she commented mischievously.

'Indeed we shall,' Jake agreed. He carried her to the bed and laid her gently down, then stretched out beside her. 'Shall we undress all at once, or a little at a time?' he asked, nibbling seductively at Alex's lips.

'All at once,' she answered, feeling the fires within her burning ever stronger. 'I've waited long enough.'

'So have I,' Jake agreed.

In seconds their clothes were removed and their bodies sought each other like starving souls reaching out for the only food which could sustain them. Jake was infinitely gentle and thoughtful after Alex managed to awkwardly confess that she was more of a novice than he might imagine.

'You're not disappointed?' she asked.

'Disappointed? Lord, no! It's like thinking you've found gold and then discovering it's diamonds instead,' he assured her, tenderly kissing her fears away. After that there was nothing else timid or awkward in her response, her willingness to abandon herself to him complete. She soon found that what they had begun that day at the Fosters' was only a small taste of the pleasures that were awaiting her when Jake felt truly free to love her completely.

'I just couldn't go on, without being able to tell you of my love,' he said, when afterwards she asked him why he had stopped that night. 'It made it something cheap and clandestine. And I didn't think you felt truly comfortable about it, in spite of what you said.'

'But why couldn't you tell me?' Alex asked, still feeling strangely out of the real world at now finding herself in Jake's arms, her cheek against his shoulder, her hand caressing his hair back from his forehead. Did he really, truly belong to her? 'Was it ... something to do with Lorna?'

Jake smiled wryly and kissed Alex's ear. 'Yes, in a way. I did "steal" Lorna from Dad, but only to keep him from making a terrible mistake, not because I wanted her for myself. And then, when I fell in love with you, I couldn't tell you because . . . well, because I'm a funny sort of person, I guess.'

'What do you mean?'

'I mean that once I'd told you I loved you, I couldn't have gone on trying to keep Lorna interested in me, and I still wasn't sure that Dad didn't want her back. You see,' he went on as Alex looked puzzled, 'I'm afraid I fell for you at about the same time I fell off the ledge into the bass pool. Even if I'd told you the story and you'd agreed to let me carry on the game, which I doubt you would have . . .'

He laughed as Alex interrupted with a 'You're darn right I wouldn't!'

'Anyway, I could never have done it convincingly. I was in heaven when I discovered I could at least bring you here to work with me, and then when your mother came into the picture I knew I had to keep up the pretence and give Dad time to decide that Darlene was the one for him. Once I saw that was a possibility, I didn't want to do anything to ruffle the waters. I just wish now we'd ended that silly quarrel sooner, because from what Dad told me, he'd lost interest in Lorna some time ago. After I realised that you were in love with me, it almost killed me to keep hurting you.'

'There were times when I thought it might kill me, too,' Alex said, snuggling against Jake's neck. 'I could take it while I thought it was helping Mother, but now that she's married your father, I'm not sure I could have just stood by and let you marry Lorna. And I definitely wasn't going to let you marry anyone else without a fight.' She looked up as Jake chuckled softly.

'So that's what's in that letter,' he said.

Alex nodded, her eyes brimming with laughter. 'I applied for a more suitable position with Mr Jake Jensen. I guess I have it now!'

'Indeed you have,' Jake agreed, feathering a tickling trail of kisses across Alex's bosom. 'Would you like to know how that ridiculous quote got started?' At Alex's nod he went on. 'It came about after I'd found out Dad was about to buy Lorna a ring. I knew she was only after his money, but I couldn't make him see it. We'd been arguing about his prospective bride's virtues one day before a ceremony we both had to attend. I was getting fed up with his defending her as if she were Joan of Arc, and while we were standing in a reception line I leaned over and said to him, "There's only one position suitable for that woman", referring only to Lorna. Unfortunately, someone overheard, and thought I'd said *a* woman, referring to women in general. I couldn't very well explain what it was really about. If Dad did make the mistake of marrying her, I didn't want to have that remark on the books as referring to my stepmother, and I had already decided to try and get her away from him if he couldn't be made to see the light any other way. She'd hardly have been receptive to my advances if she knew what I thought of her.'

'What if your father had told her?' Alex asked.

'He did, but by then I had Lorna so entranced that she thought it was just sour grapes. Besides, I denied it.'

Alex sighed. 'Poor Peter! Thank goodness he came to his senses. My mother adores him.' She looked longingly at the soft warmth of Jake's lips so close to hers, then suddenly realised that she could kiss him if she wanted and did so, smiling dreamily afterwards. 'I really don't want to do anything but make love to you for ever,' she said, 'but there's one other thing I'm curious about.'

'Let's get it over with and go back to making love,' Jake said, doing some kissing of his own.

'Why did you have that deal with Lorna about having Jenstar acquire her company? Surely you have enough charm without using that for bait. Besides, I can't believe you seriously thought that her company was a good investment. It's an out-and-out disaster.'

Jake chuckled. 'I know. But dollar signs are the only things that charm dear Lorna. That's another reason I had to get her away from Dad. She had him ready to forget everything he knows about investments and pour his own money into her company. He'd have been a pauper before she was through with him. I, on the other hand, was counting on our internal evaluation to get me off the hook, praying all the while that Dad would come to his senses before it happened. Then, when Toby Jackson fell under Lorna's spell and tried to make her company look good, I got worried. Squandering your own fortune is one thing, but doing the same with your stockholders' money is another.'

'So that's what happened to Mr Jackson!' Alex exclaimed. 'And everyone thought he was trying to please you.'

'Let's just leave it that way,' Jake said seriously. 'For Mrs Jackson's sake.'

'Of course,' Alex agreed quickly. She stroked Jake's cheek lovingly. 'You are the dearest, most thoughtful person. How soon can we be married? I know it hasn't been long, but it seems like I've been waiting for ever for you. Maybe since I was fourteen.'

Jake embraced her passionately. 'I think I have, too. How about as soon as the law allows? We can honeymoon at the farm. It should be ready by next week.'

'Perfect!' Alex exclaimed. 'I do love the farm so. It's like something from a storybook, that I've dreamed about and never thought to have.'

'I knew you felt that way,' Jake said, smiling slowly and lovingly. 'It is a perfect place for two people who aren't really crazy about city life. And it will be a perfect place for children...if there are to be children?' He raised his eyebrows questioningly at Alex.

'Oh, yes,' she replied quickly. 'Even if I have to turn part of my office into a nursery, there will be. I never thought much about it before, but looking at you...all I can think of is how much I want a little boy who looks just like you.'

'Don't forget the little girl who looks just like you,' Jake said. He sighed contentedly. 'Which one shall we work on next?'

Alex smiled at him impishly. 'You're the boss,' she said, making a move she knew already was guaranteed to arouse him. 'Is this a suitable position?'

Jake groaned and rolled over on top of her, smiling down at her with love and laughter in his eyes. 'I think,' he said, studying her thoughtfully, 'that any position you assume is suitable, as long as it's part of my life.'

CAROLE MORTIMER

JUST ONE NIGHT

Hawk Sinclair—Texas millionaire and owner of the exclusive
Sinclair hotels, determined to protect his son's inheritance.
Leonie Spencer—desperate to protect her sister's happiness.

They were together for just one night.
The night their daughter was conceived.

Blackmail, kidnapping and attempted murder add suspense
to passion in this exciting bestseller.

The success story of Carole Mortimer continues with *Just
One Night*, a captivating romance from the author of the
bestselling novels, *Gypsy* and *Merlyn's Magic*.

★

**Available in March
wherever paperbacks are sold.**

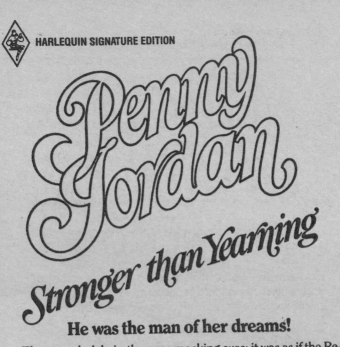

Penny Jordan

Stronger than Yearning

He was the man of her dreams!

The same dark hair, the same mocking eyes; it was as if the Regency rake of the portrait, the seducer of Jenna's dream, had come to life. Jenna, believing the last of the Deverils dead, was determined to buy the great old Yorkshire Hall—to claim it for her daughter, Lucy, and put to rest some of the painful memories of Lucy's birth. She had no way of knowing that a direct descendant of the black sheep Deveril even existed—or that James Allingham and his own powerful yearnings would disrupt her plan entirely.

Penny Jordan's first Harlequin Signature Edition *Love's Choices* was an outstanding success. Penny Jordan has written more than 40 best-selling titles—more than 4 million copies sold.

Now, be sure to buy her latest bestseller, *Stronger Than Yearning*. Available wherever paperbacks are sold—in June.

STRONG-1R

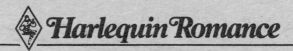
Harlequin Romance

Coming Next Month

2911 FLIRTATION RIVER Bethany Campbell
When the daughter of a U.S. senator is sent into hiding after
receiving a series of anonymous letters threatening her life,
her handsome protector provides not only safety, but a kind
of happiness she'd never known before.

2912 RECIPE FOR LOVE Kay Clifford
Vicky is stunned when the J. P. Duncan who registered for a
place in her women's summer cookery course turns out to
be a man. She soon discovers that Jay has more than cookery
on his mind!

2913 CLOUDED PARADISE Rachel Ford
Unless Catherine can get rid of the squatter living on her
beach property, she can't sell it. But Luke Devenish is
determined to stay and makes it clear that he despises rich
heiresses like Catherine.

2914 A GENTLE AWAKENING Betty Neels
Florina loves her new job as cook in the home of consultant
Sir William Sedley, and before long she realizes she loves Sir
William, too! Unfortunately Sir William is already engaged
to the glamorous but entirely unsuitable Wanda.

2915 CAPTURE A NIGHTINGALE Sue Peters
Ros doesn't really mind going to Majorca to help out the
eccentric painter Mildred Fisher. But when disaster
threatens her journey, she can't help wondering how safe
she'll be in the hands of overbearing Keel Hennessy, her
traveling companion.

2916 UNFRIENDLY ALLIANCE Jessica Steele
When Anstey is literally left holding her friend's baby, she
turns for help to the child's uncle, the powerful, forbidding
Cale Quartermaine. She isn't prepared, however, to have
Cale rearrange her life as well as the baby's!

Available in June wherever paperback books are sold, or
through Harlequin Reader Service:

In the U.S.
901 Fuhrmann Blvd.
P.O. Box 1397
Buffalo, N.Y. 14240-1397

In Canada
P.O. Box 603
Fort Erie, Ontario
L2A 5X3